I'M DOUGAL TRUMP...

WARNING!
SPIDER ON
the LOOSE!

WHERE'S MY TARANTULA?

Books by D. Trump

I'm Dougal Trump . . . and It's NOT My Fault!

I'm Dougal Trump . . . Where's My Tarantula?

I'M DOUGAL TRUMP...

SYBIL

WARNING!
SPIDER ON
the LOOSE!

WHERE'S MY TARANTULA?

BY ME, x D. TRUMP.

MACMILLAN CHILDREN'S BOOKS

First published 2013 by Macmillan Children's Books
a division of Macmillan Publishers Limited
20 New Wharf Road, London N1 9RR
Basingstoke and Oxford
Associated companies throughout the world
www.panmacmillan.com

ISBN 978-1-4472-2022-0

Text copyright © Jackie Marchant 2013
Illustrations copyright © Mike Lowery 2013

1 3 5 7 9 8 6 4 2

A CIP catalogue record for this book is available from
the British Library.

Printed and bound by CPI Group (UK) Ltd, Croydon CR0 4YY

To my favourite tarantula, Sybil – I'll never forget you.

To my unfavourite sister, Sibble – you *have* got hairy legs!

EXCITING NEWS!

I've just had a phone call from Mr Wellington, President of the London Zoological Association. One of his jobs is to rescue poor exotic creatures who have been stolen by crooks like our ex-neighbour Lysander

ABOUT the AUTHOR

Dougal Trump, known to his friends as Dougie the brilliant goalkeeper, is a good-looking boy, who attends Ocklesford Junior School.

Witzel. Sometimes Mr Wellington
asks people to look after one of
his creatures until he can return
them or find them a new home.

Today he called me to ask if I
would like to look after one of
his creatures!

He emailed me a list of
possibilities:

MIRIAM tHE
FAT-tailED GECKO

HARRIET tHE
AFRICAN Big-
EYEO Tree Frog

BILBO THE BEARDED
DRAgON

I thought Bilbo the bearded dragon looked particularly interesting. He's a lizard, not a real dragon, but he has a great beard.

Then I saw a name that leaped from the list and said *Don't look after the others, look after me!* Her name is Sybil, pronounced Sibble, just like my sister. But this Sybil is much more beautiful than my sister.

This Sybil is a rare and very large spider.

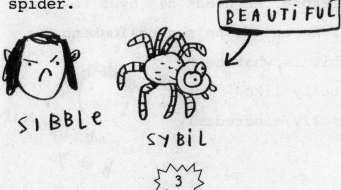

SIBBLE

SYBIL

BEAUTIFUL

Sybil is a Goliath bird-eating spider, the largest type of tarantula there is. She's the size of a dinner plate and has eight very hairy legs.

I've told Mr Wellington that Sybil is the creature for me and I can't wait until she arrives!

Comments:

SufferingSister said:
Dougal Trump is the biggest liar in history. He needs his eyes testing if he thinks he's good-looking. This is what he's really like — messy, smelly, incredibly

annoying. He's the worst brother
any sister could have. There is
absolutely NO WAY he will be
allowed to have a creature in the
house, let alone a tarantula. He
probably hasn't even asked Mum
and Dad.
Regards,
Sybil.

DAD'S NEW FIFTEEN-YEAR-OLD SPORTS CAR

Guess what? I've just had a ride in Dad's new sports car. When I say new, it's actually at least fifteen years old. He's always wanted a red Ferrari and this will be the closest he'll ever get — as the car is red, though definitely not a Ferrari.

Mum let him buy it with the last of the money Gran left when she died. Mum thought it would be a good idea if he had his own car for his window-cleaning business, but I don't think she meant him to get a sports car.

'How are you going to get your ladders on it?' she asked.

'I'll think of something,' he said. 'Fancy a spin, Dougie?'

It was great. Despite the terrible

weather we had the top down and I waved
at everyone as we went past. No one noticed
though, they were too busy trying to get
out of the rain. But I did see Angela Sweeter
dashing into Nippy News with her mum. I think
she turned round to look at me before she
went in.

Then I recognized someone standing
outside Speedy Sports. He looked up as we
went past, but I stopped waving, so I could
give him a filthy look instead. It was none

other than Stan Witzel, son of the crook Lysander who used to live next door.

When we got home, I was absolutely soaked. Dad offered Sibble a ride but she refused to get her hair wet or blown about.

'But it might improve it,' I said.

'Just because you enjoy looking like a drowned rat doesn't mean I do,' she said. 'Anyway, Mr Wellington rang and I had a nice long chat with him. Now Mum wants to know why you think you are going to bring a tarantula into the house.'

My sneaky sister has ruined my plans. Mum has told me to contact Mr Wellington and tell him that I can't have Sybil to stay after all.

'She's right,' said Dad. 'We don't need another creature in the house when we've already got you.'

Sibble thought that was the funniest thing she'd ever heard. So I contacted Mr Wellington and said he could bring Sybil the spider round whenever he wanted. I'm sure my family will love her when they see her.

MY SYBIL HAS ARRIVED!

You won't believe how beautiful she is. She's a soft brown colour with eight of the hairiest legs you've ever seen, almost as hairy as my sister Sibble's. She has two goggly

MORE ABOUT the AUTHOR

Dougal Trump plays in goal for Fairford United. The following players are lucky enough to be on the team with him:

Superspeed George Quickley, the ace winger. No one beats him to the ball.

eyes and a pair of sharp fangs.

She arrived in a big cardboard box with a sign saying *This Way Up*. Inside Sybil was sitting in a small clear box.

THIS
WAY UP

Big Bad Burt in defence. No one is brave enough to get round him.

Boing-brain Claude Barleycorn, who runs about aimlessly, confusing the opposition.

Billy Truss, whose dad is Mr Truss, the most boring teacher in the world. Billy plays in midfield and is very good at discussing tactics.

Dad was cleaning his car when Sybil arrived, which might explain why he didn't seem very interested. Mum was still at work, so she still has the pleasure of meeting the new member of our family.

Mr Wellington gave me everything I need to look after Sybil. I've also been checking the website he set up for creature lovers like me. It's called ZooBlog.

First of all, I put a thick layer of vermiculite in her big perspex tank. Then I sank the plant pot into the corner for Sybil to make her burrow. The plant pot has its bottom missing and I put it on

its side, so I can peek through
the back of her tank and see her
in there. I've filled her water
dish and now she has
everything she needs.
Once she's settled,
I'm going to give
her a snack.

Tarantulas like a warm, sunny spot.
I've been given a special lamp to
shine on her tank, but I've also
found the perfect windowsill for
her. You see, there is a bedroom in
our house with a notice on the door
that says

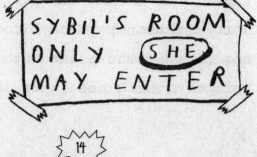

SYBIL'S ROOM
ONLY SHE
MAY ENTER

This room has a deep windowsill, which happens to be the sunniest spot in the whole house. Once I'd cleared off all the nail varnishes and other rubbish, it was the perfect spot for Sybil!

Comments:

Superspeed said:
Cool blog, Dougie! Can't wait to see Sybil. Is she a tarantula or a spider?

DynamoDougie said:
'Tarantula' is the word for a big hairy spider. They don't come much bigger and hairier than Sybil. So she is both a spider and a tarantula.

BigBadBurt said:

Will the bird-eating spider eat my mum's budgie?

BoingBrain said:

It's me — Claude. What's vermiculite?

TrussBilly said:

Although a bird-eating spider was once found eating a tiny hummingbird (which is what gave them their name), these spiders mostly eat small mice and crickets. Vermiculite is another name for hydrated laminar magnesium-aluminium-iron silicate, a naturally occurring mineral, which my mum uses for her pot plants.

It has the benefit of not going
mouldy.

DynamoDougie said:
Vermiculite is the stuff in Sybil's
tank.

SufferingSister said:

A Most UNFair Grounding

I've been grounded by my mean and unreasonable parents. It all happened (a) because Mum left a broom lying around,

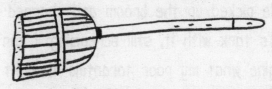

(b) because my horrible sister is scared of the incy-winciest teeniest spider, and (c) because Dad never gets round to doing things – like mending Sibble's rotting window.

This is what happened.

Sybil the spider was delighted with her sunny new spot. She soon came out to have a wander around her tank . . . just at the moment my silly sister Sibble decided to go into her room.

You should have heard her scream.

But it wasn't her scream that had me rushing to see what was going on. It was the sound of splintering wood and smashing glass.

Mum had left her broom on the landing, after using it to clear away some cobwebs. Sibble picked up the broom and charged at Sybil's tank with it, still screaming. I can't imagine what my poor tarantula thought when she saw this mad girl attacking her with a broom.

The broom slammed into Sybil's tank and the tank slammed against the window. That was when I heard the sound of breaking wood and smashing glass. I rushed into her room – in time to see the window break, the frame give way and the whole lot go flying out: window frame, glass, broom, Sybil's cage and all.

Luckily, Dad's new car broke her fall.

Unluckily, Dad was still cleaning it at the time.

Luckily, he was standing back and

admiring his car when Sybil came flying out in her tank. Thank goodness perspex is very strong, so it didn't break when it landed, corner first, on the bonnet of Dad's car.

Despite being the heaviest spider in the world, Sybil doesn't weigh that much, so she was unhurt by her fall, although she was a bit quivery for a while and had to spend some time redoing her burrow.

Dad doesn't understand that being hit by a falling broom is probably better than having the corner of a perspex tank land on your head. He grounded me. Forever. And I'm supposed to pay not only for the damage to his car, but for a new window for Sibble, by washing Mum's car until further notice. I'm not allowed to wash Dad's car – only Dad can do that.

'But you can't ground me!' I protested. 'I'm a local hero!'

'You're about as heroic as a peanut-butter sandwich,' he said.

'And it's all Sibble's fault!' I cried. 'She threw my spider and the broom out of the window! What will Mr Wellington say?'

'Mr Wellington is a fool if he thinks you are responsible enough to look after anything for more than two seconds,' said Dad. 'That spider has already gone plunging to its death.'

'She has not,' I said. 'Look.' Poor Sybil was dashing around in her tank, looking very much alive.

That was when Mum arrived home from work. Now I know where Sibble gets her screaming from.

During Mum's screaming, I heard the following words: *spider, never, that thing, no, out, take it away, Mr Wellington, Raymond* and *what?!* Plus some other words that she started but didn't finish. I decided to take poor Sybil upstairs before Mum's screaming upset her too much.

Mum made Dad telephone Mr Wellington to say we weren't having Sybil in the house. I listened in from the landing and this is what I heard Dad say:

YES, ThAt's Right, Mr Wellington, I DiD SAY thAt. OF COURSe, GOOD-BYe.

'What did he say?' asked Mum. 'When is he coming to take that thing away?'

'Well, it appears I agreed to let Dougie have his tarantula,' said Dad.

Mum did a bit more screaming, during which I heard the words *what*, *why* and *you idiot!*

Apparently, Dad told Mr Wellington that she was a welcome addition to our family and he was planning to make sure she was very well cared for. When Dad said 'she', he meant his car – but Mr Wellington thought he meant Sybil!

NOTES FROM DOUGIE'S PIT

More News of Sybil

After a very unfortunate incident involving a window, a broom and a screaming mother, Sybil is now safe in the corner of my bedroom under my dormer window.

More ABOUT the AUTHOR

Dougal is writing this blog in his new loft room, using the computer that was his reward for being a local hero.*

* If you don't yet know how I became a local hero, the

27

As soon as Sybil has calmed down, I'm going to give her a tasty snack from the box of live crickets Mr Wellington gave me.

whole amazing story is in my first book — I'm Dougal Trump . . . and It's NOT My Fault!

I spend a lot of time lying on the floor watching her in her burrow. Mostly she just sits there, completely still but for the occasional twitch of her fangs.

But I know she'll spring to life as soon as she sees her dinner walking past her burrow — I can't wait.

Comments:

SweetAngieBabe said:
Dougie, please stop going on about having a giant tarantula in your room — we're not interested and we don't believe you. And don't you ever try and kiss me again.

BigBadBurt said:
Did you really try and kiss Angela Sweeter?

DynamoDougie said:
It was a long time ago and Angela has never forgotten it. Now, I really must go and see how my new eight-legged friend is getting on. Goodnight.

IhateDougie said:

I'm watching you, Dougal Trump.

Await instructions.

What happens if you can't stand your mum's cooking

The only time I'm allowed out of my room, apart from breakfast and going to school, is when I have to come down and eat Mum's brown goo, which is the stuff she serves up for dinner. I'd be very happy to stay in my room all day with Sybil and not go to school and not eat brown goo, but my unreasonable parents won't let me.

Mum doesn't understand that I do try my hardest to eat her brown goo. Unfortunately, she caught me as I was passing a particularly nasty-looking lump under the table to the dog last night.

This meant that, as well as forcing down the brown goo, I had to listen to a lecture from Mum and Dad about what an ungrateful son I am, and watch Sibble nodding smugly all the way through. On and on they went, about how hard they work to put food on the table and how Mum spends ages trying to find nice things for me to eat. I would have given her a list of all the things I like, which does not include brown goo, but I couldn't get a word in.

In the end, I just sat there going *Yes, Mum* every now and then until she stopped. Then she was looking at me, the way Mr Truss does when he's expecting an answer.

'Yes, Mum,' I said.

Sibble snorted.

I had no idea what I'd agreed to until I asked Mum what was for dinner tonight, so I could prepare the poor dog.

'Don't you remember what you agreed to last night?' she said. 'As you don't like my cooking, you are cooking your own dinners from now on!'

RESULT!!

NOTES FROM DOUGIE'S PIT

THE AWESOME BLOG OF DOUGAL TRUMP

| HOME | BLOG | LINKS | CONTACT |

DOUGIE'S DELICIOUS BAKED-BEAN PIZZA

You Will Need:

ONE PIZZA BASE

ONE CAN BAKED BEANS

SOME GRATED Cheese

MORE ABOUT the AUTHOR

Dougal shares his loft room with an old hamster, a spider called Ida, who lives in the top corner, and a tarantula called Sybil, who lives in the bottom corner.

Method:

Put beans and cheese on pizza base, cook and eat. Yum!

Comments:

Superspeed said:
Delicious, Dougie! Not enough to go round though.

SweetAngieBabe said:
Sounds absolutely revolting — just like you.

TrussBilly said:
Could you be more specific with the quantities of ingredients?

SufferingSister said:

Mum says it won't be long before you're begging her to cook for you again. And you left a horrible mess in the kitchen.

BoingBrain said:

Mum says I shouldn't have made your recipe without the pizza base, but I couldn't find one. The beans went all over the oven and made it smoke. Mum is on her hands and knees trying to clean it.

BigBadBurt said:

My mum says I should have opened the can of beans first. It exploded in the oven

and the beans went everywhere.
The pizza base got so burnt it
caught fire. Mum's just called the
fire brigade. I'm going have to
evacuate, bye.

IhateDougie said:
Go to the hollow tree after school
and look inside. Make sure you are
alone. Now delete this comment.

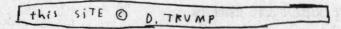

A tARANtulA Eating A cricket

I took absolutely no notice of the silly comment from *IhateDougie*. And I forgot to look in the hollow tree anyway. That's because of all the excitement on the way home — I was bringing everyone to meet Sybil and watch her eat her first cricket.

By 'everyone' I mean George, Burt, Claude and Billy. I asked Angela Sweeter too but she said no way was she coming home with a bunch of boys to look at a tarantula eating a cricket. Strange girl.

We all lay on our fronts on the floor and, after a bit of wriggling to get comfortable in the mess, settled down to peer into Sybil's burrow.

39

'She's not doing much,' said George.

'I can only see her hairy bottom,' said Burt. 'I wanted to count her eyes.'

'Shh,' I whispered. 'She's still settling in. But she might come out for a cricket.'

Using the long tweezers that Mr Wellington had given me, I took a cricket out of the box and put it in Sybil's tank. Everyone peered over the top to see if she'd come out to get it. Nothing happened. Sybil just stayed all quiet and innocent in her burrow. I thought she probably wasn't hungry after all, then – WHAM!

It was the coolest thing. Sybil was so fast we barely saw her. She came out, grabbed the cricket and went back again. The cricket didn't stand a chance – one nip from Sybil and it was paralysed and helpless. She injected acid into it to turn its insides into goo, which she could suck up with her own special straw (I knew this is what she was doing from what I'd read on ZooBlog). Then she settled down quietly with her dinner.

'She likes to make it last,' I said, 'so let's leave her in peace.'

I let the boys feed Sybil's crickets. They eat mealworms, which are like large maggots, all squirmy and wriggly. I've got a whole box of them on my desk.

'What do the mealworms eat?' asked Claude.

'Bug grub and old potatoes,' I said as we watched them wriggling about. They are the easiest creatures to look after – even Claude could do it.

'Does your mum mind you keeping crickets and mealworms in your room?' asked Billy.

'Mum won't come in my room now that Sybil's here so I can keep what I like. But I have to keep the mice in the freezer.' That's something else Mr Wellington gave me, a bag of frozen mice for Sybil.

'Does your mum know you're keeping mice in the freezer?' asked George.

'Of course not,' I said. 'I've hidden them in an ice-cream container. And I've told Mum that Sybil eats giant flies.'

'My mum would go mad if I kept mice in the freezer,' said George.

'I ate a slug once,' said Claude, ending the conversation.

NOTES FROM DOUGIE'S PIT

THE AWESOME BLOG OF DOUGAL TRUMP

| HOME | BLOG | LINKS | CONTACT |

Dougie's House Rules

this is A (PRIVATE) BLOG, For PRIViLeGED memBers Of Dougie's iNNer circLe **ONLY**. No ONe else is allowed NeAr it.

more ABOUT the AUTHOR

Unfortunately poor Dougal has to share his house with his unreasonable parents and his moany sister, who is the bane of his life.

SufferingSister said:
Privileged? Laugh out loud.

Superspeed said:
How come your sister is on this blog? Is she privileged?

DynamoDougie said:
Sibble has the privilege of being my sister. The problem is, she has no idea how lucky she is.

BoingBrain said:
Am I privileged? What's a bane?

DynamoDougie said:
You are all privileged. A bane is a pain, only worse. See you at football later.

Superspeed said:

Great football training tonight!
How come you weren't there, Dougie?

DynamoDougie said:

I was on my way out, when Sibble
reminded me I'd been grounded, in
such a loud voice that Mum heard.

IhateDougie said:

You were supposed to look in the
hollow tree. You have one more
chance to do as I ask. Look
inside the hollow tree or else.
Now delete this comment.

TOP
TENS
PICS
TWITTER

IMPORTANT SECURITY ANNOUNCEMENT

CLAUDE

After being up half the night trying to work it out, I have now put a cunning password system in place.
I will reveal the password to my inner circle today.
Must dash — I'm late for school.

MORE ABOUT the AUTHOR

Dougal also owns a pet worm called Claude, who lives under his bed on a saucer with some damp earth. Worms spend their days eating soil and pooing it out the other end. Dougie

47

Has anyone seen my
trainers?

Comments:

Superspeed said:
Cool password, Dougie!

is waiting
to see how
long it takes
Claude to
turn all the
earth into
poo, and
whether he
will turn
round and eat
it all again.

BigBadBurt said:
Could we have
another recipe?

TrussBilly said:
Is your password an accurate
description of your sister?

SweetAngieBabe said:
I don't think your sister will like
your password.

BoingBrain said:

I forgot the password, so I wrote it on my hand.

SufferingSister said:

How dare you use that as your password — I DO NOT HAVE HAIRY LEGS!!

IhateDougie said:

So the password's *SisterHairyLegs*. I hope you weren't trying to keep me away. If you want your trainers back, look in the hollow tree like I asked you.

THE Mice AND
My trainers

I changed my password and gave it to my
friends the next day. I even gave it to
Angela Sweeter, because
she kept asking for it.

As we went past the
hollow tree on the way home
from school, I put my hand in
the hole. And sure enough,
there were my trainers.

I was still staring at them when Burt
grabbed them off me and started a game of
rugby with them. They nearly ended up in the
River Ockle, so we switched to football. Then
basketball. Then Claude said we should play ping-
pong with them, but we were nearly off the
fields by then. I hadn't been home long when

I heard a bloodcurdling scream coming from the freezer. By that I mean from where the freezer is in the kitchen. I ran down to find Sibble gagging over an ice-cream container.

'Those are for my spider,' I said. 'She likes mice.'

'You are SO going to be grounded forever for this,' she said. Her voice was quiet and her lips were all quivery.

'Only if you tell,' I said.

'I am SO going to tell,' she said. A little louder this time.

'I'll let Sybil run around in the bath if you tell,' I said.

'I bet you'll do that anyway,' she said.

'OK. I'll put one of Sybil's live crickets down your neck.'

'You think I'd ever let my horrible little dork of a brother get that close to me?'

She stepped back to make her point.

'I'm still telling Mum.' I tried Threat Number Three.

'I'll tip my box of live mealworms into your room.'

'Mealworms?'

'You know, like maggots only bigger. And vegetarian.'

'I don't believe you.'

She went up to her room. A minute later I came in with my box of mealworms. With the lid off.

I didn't throw them in her room though. I just let her look at them, for long enough to go a bit pale and promise that she wouldn't tell Mum about the mice in the freezer. Which wasn't very long. Then I made her promise to stay away from my blog.

That's how you deal with big sisters.

Dougie's Oreo Skyscraper

You Will Need:

- One packet Oreo biscuits
- One jar peanut butter

MORE ABOUT the AUTHOR

Dougal's dad is a window cleaner. The other day he was arrested for carrying a dangerous load. He'd put his ladders on his sports car and dangled the bucket on the end of them.

Method:

Carefully stick all the Oreos together in a skyscraper, using a generous dollop of peanut butter between each one as glue.

Comments:

BoingBrain said:

We don't have any Oreos, so I used custard creams instead.
Is that OK?

TrussBilly said:

I'm finding it difficult to keep it straight. It looks more like the Leaning Tower of Pisa.

BigBadBurt said:

Mine keeps falling over — what should I do?

DynamoDougie said:

Call it an Oreo Log.

BigBadBurt said:

But it hasn't got Oreos in it. I had to use Bourbons.

DynamoDougie said:

Then call it a Bourbon Log.

BigBadBurt said:

It's too square for a log.

DynamoDougie said:

Bourbon Brick?

IhateDougie said:

So you got your trainers back. Now I'm going to give you one more warning. Then you'll know I mean business, and you will do exactly what I tell you.

HELP!!
DISASTER!

Something truly horrible and terrible has happened. Something so awful that it is hard to put into words. But I will try.

Sybil has gone!

Not my sister. If that happened I wouldn't be upset at all.

My beautiful eight-legged Goliath bird-eating spider Sybil has gone. Vanished. Perspex tank and all.

As soon as I came home from school, I went straight upstairs to tell Sybil about my day. I was going to tell her how Mr Truss said we weren't allowed footballs in the playground because they're dangerous. About how we walked home over the fields, seeing

how many times we could
bounce the ball off
Claude's head. How I saw
a large silver car going
down our street, which

I'm sure was driven by none other than that
crook Lysander Witzel.

I was going to give Sybil the mouse I'd
sneaked out of the freezer to defrost while
I was at school.

But Sybil wasn't there. There was only
her lamp, which was shining over the scrape
marks where her tank had been. I ran
straight downstairs, where I found Mum in the
kitchen, preparing her brown goo.

'Mum! Have you seen Sybil?'

'She's not back from school yet, is she?'

'I don't mean her! I mean my beautiful
Sybil with eight hairy legs.'

She shuddered. '*That* Sybil is anything but beautiful. I don't know how I can bear having her in the house.'

I searched the whole house. By the time I'd finished, Mum had put the brown goo in the oven to froth and was in the living room reading the *Ocklesford Gazette*. I came in, frantic.

'For goodness sake, Dougie, what is the matter with you?'

'I told you – Sybil has gone!'

'Sybil is in her room doing her homework, like you should be doing instead of charging round the house.'

'I mean the nice Sybil with eight hairy legs, not the horrible Sibble with two hairy legs.'

Mum went pale. 'When you asked me whether I'd seen your giant tarantula, I assumed you meant had I ever seen her? That *is* what you meant, isn't it, Dougie?'

'Mum,' I sighed, 'Sybil the rare Goliath bird-eating spider is no longer in my room.'

Mum made a funny noise, a sort of cross between a cough and a gurgle. With a touch of squeak. Then she screamed.

When Dad came home, she was standing on the coffee table, still screeching her head off, while the dog ran round barking.

'Christabel,' said Dad, 'why are you screaming on the coffee table, why is the *Ocklesford Gazette* all over the floor and why can't you stop the dog from making that infernal racket?'

'The thing has escaped, Ray! There's a plate-sized tarantula on the loose in the house! Help!'

'Dougie?' growled Dad, in that way he does when everything is bound to be my fault.

'Her tank has gone,' I said. 'I've searched the house and I can't find it.'

'It's probably buried under the heap of rubbish on the floor in that pit of a room of yours,' said Dad. 'Have you looked?'

'Yes. Her tank is not in the house.'

'Are you sure she was in it?'

That was a silly thing to say. Mum jumped from the coffee table on to the kitchen table, to do more shrieking. I told her not to worry, because if Sybil had got out of her tank before it went missing, she would stay out of the way in a dark corner and only come out to pounce. Mum screamed even more. I left her to it and started to search all the dark places in the house Sybil might have hidden in.

I was deep into the hall cupboard, when Sibble came downstairs. 'Get out of my way, and why are you putting rubbish everywhere, you stupid little twerp?' she said.

'I'm trying to find your namesake,' I said. 'She's gone walkies. She could be anywhere, waiting to pounce.'

You should have heard her scream.

But it was no good. Sybil's tank had gone and I knew deep down that she was in it.

She could be anywhere.

NOTES FROM DOUGIE'S PIT

THE AWESOME BLOG OF DOUGAL TRUMP

| HOME | BLOG | LINKS | CONTACT |

MISSING!

ONE goliath Bird-
Eating SPIDER

Pale golden Brown,
8 VERY
HAIRY
legs.

ABOUT the size
of a plate.

ANSWERS to the NAME:

→ SYBIL ←

IF FOUND please contact
DOUGAL TRUMP immediately!

65

Has anyone seen my tarantula? I'll do anything to get her back.

more ABOUT the AUTHOR

Dougal Trump is far too upset to say any more about himself today.

Comments:

TrussBilly said:
Are you sure you've looked everywhere? She can't have disappeared just like that.

BoingBrain said:
Is she in your school bag?

BigBadBurt said:
Oh no! I was really looking forward to counting her eyes.

Superspeed said:

Don't worry, we will help you find
her.

SweetAngieBabe said:

My brother Eric is in your sister's
class and he says you really do
have a tarantula. Or did. Trust you
to lose it already. Also, your new
password is rubbish.

IhateDougie said:

If you want to see your
tarantula again, do as I ask.
Stop changing the passwords on
this blog. The password will
remain as *SibbleFanciesEric*.
Tell everyone you found your
tarantula. Go to the hollow tree

after school. Alone. You will find
something in there. Keep it until
further instructions. Now delete
this entry.

AN URGENT CONFLAB

Last night I didn't bother making myself anything to eat. I stayed in my room, staring at the spot where Sybil used to live.

On the way to school, I lied and told everyone that I'd found her in my room, lurking under my school trousers.

'Just as well,' said George. 'You wouldn't want to put your trousers on with her inside.'

They all thought that was funny. I don't think they noticed that I wasn't laughing. I thought about Sybil all morning, and Mr Truss couldn't believe how quiet I was. I even gave him a sensible answer to one of his questions. At break I didn't want to have a kick around with the ball that Burt had sneaked into the playground.

'But it was your idea,' he said. 'What's wrong with you?'

'Nothing,' I said. I couldn't tell them *IhateDougie* had taken Sybil, because he had sworn me to secrecy. Now Billy, George, Burt and Claude were all looking at me.

It was too much. I cracked and told them everything. 'I have no idea who *IhateDougie* is,' I said when I'd finished. 'Or why he – or she – has stolen Sybil.'

'Could be anyone,' said Burt, which wasn't very helpful.

'It must be someone who hates Dougie,' said Claude.

'That doesn't narrow it down very much,' said Billy.

'It must be someone who has the password to Dougie's blog,' said George. 'That means it's one of us.'

We were talking so loudly that Mrs
Minns came over to see what all the fuss
was about.

'Nothing,' I said. 'We
were just deciding whether
Manchester United, Arsenal
or Stamford United is
the best football team
in the world.'

'Brazil is the best football team in the
world,' said Mrs Minns. 'Keep the noise down.'

'Right,' whispered Billy. 'We need to go
through all the people who have access to
Dougie's blog and eliminate them one by one.'

'Eliminate?' asked Burt.

'He means eliminate from enquiries,' said
George. 'To prove it couldn't be them. All
agreed?'

'Agreed,' I said.

'Agreed,' said Billy.

'All right, agreed,' said Burt.

'I didn't know Mrs Minns supported Brazil,' said Claude.

We put our heads together and decided the following:

* Sybil was stolen while I was at school.
* Billy couldn't have stolen Sybil because he walked home with us until the crossroads, where he went off with Claude.
* George couldn't have stolen Sybil because he walked home with us until the crossroads, then went the other way with Burt.

* Burt couldn't have stolen Sybil because he was walking home with George.
* Claude couldn't have stolen Sybil because he wouldn't know how to.
* I couldn't have stolen Sybil because I love her.
* *IhateDougie* must have an accomplice.

We all went very quiet as we thought about the last point. At that moment Angela Sweeter came over and told us that break was over and Mr Truss was waiting for us to go back in.

As she went off, we all looked at each other.

'No way,' I said. 'Angela wouldn't do a thing like that.'

'What's an accomplice?' said Claude.

'Someone is helping *IhateDougie*,' said Billy.

'And it must be someone who goes on the blog,' I said, as we went into the classroom. 'Who told him the password was *SisterHairyLegs*. And then told him it had changed to *SibbleFanciesEric*.'

'Dougal Trump, please keep the noise down,' said Mr Truss.

I did my best to keep the noise down until lunch, but Mr Truss still gave me several warnings. Luckily, I wasn't kept in after class, so I had a chance to speak to Angela.

It wasn't easy to get her on her own. Why do girls have to go around in groups? Eventually I caught her outside the girls' toilets.

'I can't believe you've followed me to the girls' toilets,' she said.

'I need to speak to you. Alone. Urgently.'

'You are absolutely not going to try and kiss me ever again.'

'I don't want to kiss you. I want to talk to you.'

'Good,' she said. 'Because I might be getting a boyfriend.'

'Boyfriend?'

'Keep your voice down!' she hissed. 'It's still a secret.' And then she went in and closed the door.

While I was waiting for her to come out, three teachers asked me what I was doing there. Eventually Angela came out, with three friends. But she hung back so I could speak to her.

'Someone stole Sybil,' I whispered.

'I know, I saw your blog.'

'It has to be someone who's on the blog,' I said.

'Why? Everyone knows about your tarantula – you keep going on about it.'

'I need to eliminate you from my enquiries.'

'I didn't steal your tarantula,' she said. 'I'd rather eat one of your recipes than go near one of those disgusting spiders.' She did such a good shrug, I knew she wasn't lying. Then she ran off to catch up with her friends.

As I walked past them, I heard her say, in a very loud voice:

'Dougie Trump is most definitely not, and never will be, my boyfriend.'

What I FOUND iN the HOLLOW Tree

'Did you notice anything suspicious yesterday?'
asked Billy, as we walked home from school.

'Only Lysander Witzel driving a silver car,'
I said.

'Maybe he stole Sybil!' said Burt. 'The
fiend!'

'He doesn't know anything about Sybil,' I
said. 'He doesn't live next door any more.'

'Isn't Mr Witzel supposed to be in prison?'
asked George.

'He must have talked his way out,' I said.
'Did I tell you I saw Stan Witzel the other
day, just standing on the street corner?'

'I thought they'd moved out of the
area,' said Burt.

'Not far enough,' I said.

'Never mind all that,' said Billy. 'We need a plan. Now, what did the message from *IhateDougie* say?'

'He's going to leave me instructions on the blog. I have to delete them straight away and tell no one. And I'm supposed to pretend that Sybil isn't missing. And I've got to look in the hollow tree. Alone.'

'We'd better walk ahead then,' said Billy. 'In case he's watching.'

I let the others go ahead, then stuck my hand in the tree and brought out a small cardboard box with holes in the top. The box had a five-pound note stuck to it and a torn-off bit of paper with a message:

Keep until further instructions.
Look after it well and Sybil will be
fine. Tell anyone about this and
she'll be a seven-legged spider.
Now eat this note.

I put the box carefully in my bag. I read the note again. *Tell anyone about this and she'll be a seven-legged spider.*

He was threatening to chop off one of her legs!

I was still chewing the note when I caught up with the others. I had to think very carefully about what to say to them. Sybil's legs depended on it.

'It was just another note.' I swallowed. 'It said – er – oh dear,

I can't remember what it said. Never mind, I'm sure he'll send another one.'

'Or she,' said Burt.

'It's not Angela,' I said.

'What about your sister?' said George.

'There is no way she could have done it,' I said. 'She's terrified of the inciest, winciest spider.'

'Then who?' said Claude.

That was the most sensible question Claude has ever asked. But none of us had an answer.

What was in the

As soon as I got home, I went up to my room and took the box out of my bag. I carefully peeled the fiver away from the tape and lifted the lid. When I saw what was in there, I nearly dropped the box.

Two big bulgy eyes stared up at me. Under that was an enormous grinning mouth. A huge fat belly and a green slimy body with bumps all over it. It was the biggest frog I'd ever  seen. It was about the size of a deflated football and looked a bit like Burt.

I went on to ZooBlog to see if someone could identify what it was. After several messages and lots of descriptions, I now know that what I have is a giant African bullfrog. I've decided to call him Burt.

I don't know how long he was in the hollow tree for. He definitely wasn't in there yesterday when I pulled my trainers out, but he could have been there all night, lonely in the dark. Still, he's got me to look after him now.

I cleaned out an old fish tank and found some compost in a bag at the end of the garden. Then I had to find a water container for Burt to sit in. The most suitable one was in the freezer, full of ice cream. So I ate the ice cream and filled the container up with water.

I was just carrying it upstairs when

Sibble threw open her bedroom door and rushed out at me.

'Why are you carrying water upstairs?' she yelled. 'And who said you could finish the ice cream?'

'I'm doing my own dinners, remember?' I said. 'And this is for my mealworms to have a swim about in. Would you like to watch?'

She went pale again and stepped back into her room. I carried the water into my room, shut the door and got Burt's new home ready. I put the tub of water into the tank and then lined the tank with Mum's compost. I carefully lifted Burt in and replaced the lid, then put a couple of heavy books on top of the lid to prevent him from jumping out.

I hope Burt likes his new home.

African bullfrogs eat crickets, so it's just as well I still have a box of them on

83

my desk. They eat mice as well, and I've got
a whole load of them in another ice-cream
container in the freezer. Plus the one I
defrosted for Sybil yesterday.

I hope Sybil is all right.

HOW to CLEAN YOUR MUM'S CAR

You Will Need:

ONE HOSE

ONE BUCKET OF SOAPY WATER

ONE LARGE sponge

85

Method:

Spread soapy water all over car with sponge. Spray with hose. See how much water you can get in your sister's boarded-up window, which Dad still hasn't fixed. Demand a tenner towards the repair of Sibble's window, which you have been unfairly made to pay for.

MORE ABOUT the AUTHOR

When he's grounded, or supposed to be doing homework, Dougal likes to look out of the window of his loft room and see what his neighbours are up to. On one side he can see a garden with grass nearly as long as in his own garden. This is the Witzel house, which

Comments:

BoingBrain said:
I tried the hose but
no water came out.

DynamoDougie said:
Did you connect the
hose to a tap?

BoingBrain said:
Your recipe didn't
say that.

has been
for sale
since Dougal
discovered
the Witzels
were a bunch
of crooks.
Dougal's mum
is very cross
because they
chose to
use a rival
estate agent
instead of
the one she
works for.

DynamoDougie said:
I didn't say to shut the car
windows either. It's obvious.

BoingBrain said:

Oh. Now the inside of the car is soaking wet.

BigBadBurt said:

When I asked for another recipe, I meant something you can eat.

DynamoDougie said:

If you want something to eat, just hunt around in the car, especially down the back of the seats or under the seat in front. You'll find lots to eat — half a snack bar or an unfinished bag of crisps, for example.

IhateDougie said:

I hope you didn't tell anyone about
what you found in the hollow tree.
Await instructions.

DynamoDougie said:

Is Sybil all right?

THE WiTZeL HOUse

Despite staying up last night and constantly checking my blog, there was nothing more from *IhateDougie*. Nothing after I'd watched Burt eat a couple of crickets, nothing after I'd fallen asleep over my keyboard and nothing this morning.

'We're coming round to yours today, aren't we?' said Billy, as we were on our way home.

'Of course,' I said, suddenly remembering. I made everyone go straight into the garden — I didn't want them to find Burt the bullfrog in my room.

'Oh, Dougie,' said Mum, coming outside. 'I think I should tell the police about your missing spider. People ought to know there's a dangerous tarantula on the loose. And you should tell Mr Wellington at the Zoological Association.'

'It's all right,' I said. 'I found her. She was safe in my room after all, hiding under some clothes.'

Mum muttered something about me being the limit and shut the back door. Then she opened it again to let the dog out. Luckily he went sniffing down the even wilder end of the garden and didn't spot George finding my football in the long grass.

SNIFF
SNIFF

'Dougie's in goal!' George yelled, kicking the ball towards me. It thumped against the fence, making it rattle.

'Wide,' I said with a grin, carrying the ball further down the garden, so we could use the fence as a goal. I threw the ball and Billy and George had a tussle for it. Then the dog got fed up with sniffing around and joined in, jumping and barking and trying to snatch the ball. Burt did a great defensive move and the ball shot off, through a hole in the bottom of the fence and into the Witzel garden – followed by the dog.

Followed by me. It was a bit of a squeeze.

'Give that ball back, you stupid mutt!' I yelled, as he ran around the Witzel garden with my ball deflating in his mouth.

'Go, Dougie!' Burt shouted over the fence.

'Missed again!' said George, as I made a desperate grab for the dog.

'You might find it easier if you . . .' Billy gave some instruction I couldn't hear.

'Who are those people?' said Claude.

I stopped chasing the dog. Three people had just come out of the Witzels' back door. A tall, cross-looking man, an older boy who didn't look like he'd be any good at football and Mum's rival estate agent, Sarah.

'And this is the garden,' said Sarah. I'm sure they'd never have guessed.

'And who is that?' said the man, looking at me. 'He doesn't come with the house, does he?'

'Oh no!' Sarah laughed, glaring at me. 'I think he lives next door.'

The man scowled at me. Then he scowled at the dog, who was standing there with his

94

tail wagging and a deflated football in his mouth. 'Well, I do rather like the house.' He looked over to our garden and saw four boys staring at him over the fence. 'But I'm not sure about the neighbours.'

When he looked back, the dog had dropped the ball and started doing a great big poo.

Which gave me the perfect opportunity to grab the ball. 'Just getting my ball back,' I said. I could feel the man's eyes on me as I walked innocently back to the fence.

Unfortunately, the hole wasn't so visible from that side and while I was looking for it the dog sneaked up behind me and grabbed the ball. So I had to go chasing him again, while Sarah, the man and the boy looked on and George, Billy, Burt and Claude cheered.

By the time I got the ball back, I'd trodden in the poo and it was all over the garden and all over my shoes.

That was when the back door opened and two more people came out of the Witzel house. A woman and a girl.

The girl was Angela Sweeter.

'We like the house,' said her mum.

'No, we don't,' said Angela, looking at me.

HOW TO
CLEAN YOUR DAD'S CAR

You Will Need:

- Triple Wax
- High Performance Glass Cleaner
- Special Sporty Car Polish
- Special Sporty Car Shampoo
- Special Sporty Car Conditioner

MORE ABOUT the AUTHOR

On the other side from the Witzels' is a very neat garden. This belongs to the house where Mrs Grim lives with her precious cat, who is called Precious. You hardly see Precious, because he is too precious to be let outside.

- Blackening Wheel Cleaner
- Alloy Wheel Spray
- Dashboard wipes, in three smells
- Air freshener for the hoover
- UPVC cleaner
- One can beer
- Several tea towels
- Fluffy sheepskin glove
- Shammy leather
- Hoover
- Bucket of warm water, at just the right temperature
- One can Coke
- Three packets crisps
- One pair earplugs
- One pair heels for kicking

Method:
- Run around finding all the

above ingredients for your dad.

- Kick your heels while he makes you watch him put them all to use, describing in tedious detail how each one will enhance the performance of his car.
- Drink your Coke while he drinks the beer.
- Eat your crisps as far away as possible, so you don't get any crumbs on his car. Keep your greasy fingers away from it.
- Put earplugs in when Mum realizes Dad's been using her best tea towels to dry his car.
- Refuse to be blamed for being the one who gave him those tea towels.

Comments:

TrussBilly said:
You spell it 'chamois leather', not 'shammy leather'. The proper kind is made from the leather of the chamois goat. Or are you using a fake kind?

DynamoDougie said:
For my dad's car? Nothing but the best.

Superspeed said:
What was that I saw in the corner of your room? That great ugly thing you called Burt?

SweetAngieBabe said:
That was probably Burt.

Superspeed said:

Ah, so that's what happened to Burt.
Angela kissed him and he turned into
the biggest, ugliest frog you've
ever seen. Are you going to kiss him
again to turn him back?

SweetAngieBabe said:

I did not kiss Burt and I don't
know what you are talking about.
I don't even know why I'm on this
blog. Goodbye.
PS — Dougie, could you ask your
sister what nail varnish she was
wearing when she came home with
Eric after school today?

DynamoDougie said:
Sibble says she didn't go home with
Eric after school and it's called
Pink Razzle Dazzle or something.

BigBadBurt said:
Are you saying I look like a frog?

SuperSpeed said:
There was definitely something big
and ugly in your room today.

DynamoDougie said:
Oh, you mean Sibble! Yes, she
did pop into my room to tell me
about the pink nail varnish and to
deny that she went home with Eric
Sweeter. Goodnight, everyone.

IhateDougie said:

Oh dear — your friends all seem
to know about the bullfrog. Poor
Sybil.

DynamoDougie said:

Please don't hurt Sybil! I'll do
anything!

IhateDougie said:

Good — await instructions.

BURT the BULLfrog and Mrs GRIM

I'm finding it very hard to keep quiet about Burt the African bullfrog. The thing is, he's really great. Giving him the mouse that I'd defrosted for Sybil was awesome.

I dangled the mouse over him and for a moment, he just sat there, doing nothing but the occasional blink and gulp. Then – bam! It was brilliant. He leaped forward and grabbed the mouse in his great big mouth. With two chews and a gulp the mouse had all gone, apart from its tail, which was still sticking out of Burt's mouth.

He sat there for a while and then, with a lift of his head, down went the tail. I'm sure he looked at me to say *Thanks, that was delicious*. His big mouth has an even wider grin now.

I like Burt. But I miss Sybil.

I sat in my room feeling glum and looking out of the window. Mrs Grim was in her garden, picking up all her gnomes and putting them in her shed. She was humming to herself, which meant she was in a good mood.

Suddenly her cat Precious came shooting out of her house – a huge ball of spiky white fluff. Followed by a dog. A big soppy Labrador-type thing, who ran after the cat.

And then Mrs Grim did the strangest thing of all.

She laughed.

A dog was chasing her precious cat down the garden and Mrs Grim was throwing her head back and letting out that screechy laugh of hers.

Then the dog forgot all about the cat and started sniffing around the flowers, while Mrs Grim just stood there without telling it off.

Then it got even more interesting. A man came out of the house. Mrs Grim rushed up to him, he took her arm and they went wandering around the garden together. They

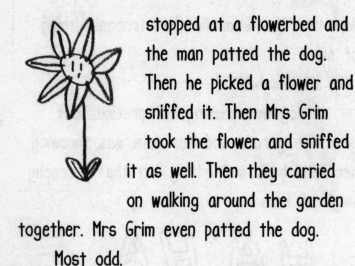

stopped at a flowerbed and
the man patted the dog.
Then he picked a flower and
sniffed it. Then Mrs Grim
took the flower and sniffed
it as well. Then they carried
on walking around the garden
together. Mrs Grim even patted the dog.
Most odd.

NOTES FROM DOUGIE'S PIT

THE AWESOME BLOG OF DOUGAL TRUMP

| HOME | BLOG | LINKS | CONTACT |

OVEN CHIP
AND KETCHUP
MOUNTAIN

You Will Need:

- One packet oven chips
- One bottle tomato ketchup

Method:

Place oven chips in a bowl, pour tomato ketchup over and mix thoroughly.

MORE ABOUT the AUTHOR

Dougal Trump is turning into a good cook. He is thinking about writing a book of recipes — if he can find the time.

Comments:

TrussBilly said:
This also works with microwave chips. By the way, you need to cook the chips before eating.

BoingBrain said:
Mum made the Oven Chip and Ketchup Mountain for me. She didn't know which size bottle of ketchup to use, so she found the biggest. You couldn't see the chips in all the ketchup and I had to fish around for them. Now I feel sick.

BigBadBurt said:
My bag of chips caught fire and
Mum had to call the fire brigade
again.

BoingBrain said:
I've just been sick. It was all
red.

TrussBilly said:
I hope you will be all right
for tomorrow's match against
Highton Wanderers. Dougie, do you
remember what we discussed about
tactics? You didn't seem to be
listening.

DynamoDougie said:
I know my tactics. Stop the ball

from going in the back of the net
every time Burt lets it through
defence.

IhateDougie said:
Leave Burt in the hollow tree
before the match tomorrow. Don't
let anyone see you. Or else. Delete
this message RIGHT NOW!

DynamoDougie said:
Can I have Sybil back now?

IhateDougie said:
Do as you are told, or you will
have her back one leg at a time.
Delete this message as well.

DynamoDougie said:

Is she all right? She is due for a
mouse. I fed hers to Burt.

IhateDougie said:

Sybil will get nothing unless you
do exactly as I say.

The MATCH AND the hollow tree

We lost our match against Highton Wanderers and everyone is blaming me. It's not my fault I didn't see the ball coming because I was looking over at the hollow tree.

I was worried about Burt. I'd carefully put him back in the box he came in, then sprayed his back with water to keep him nice and moist, before sneaking him back into the hollow tree.

Tom, our coach, told me off for not listening to his team talk. He knew I wasn't

listening because when he asked me a question, I said, 'Burt.'

How was I to know that the question he'd asked was who was the smallest and fastest person in our team?

At half-time, Tom said it would be quite helpful if I didn't let any more goals in. George was doing his best by scoring at the other end, but it was hard to keep up.

At full-time, Tom said it would have been quite helpful if I hadn't let any more goals in. We lost 6-3.

But it was hard to concentrate when I couldn't stop thinking about Burt stuck in the tree and the fact that I have no idea where Sybil is.

Dad watched the second half and walked me home. 'It would have been good if you hadn't let so many goals in,' he observed.

We'd just got in when our doorbell went *clunk*. The reason our doorbell goes *clunk* is because it's another thing Dad still hasn't fixed. I wish he'd spend more time fixing things and less time watching me play football so he can complain if I let any goals in.

Mrs Grim was at the door, together with the man I'd seen in her garden. I thought she'd come to complain about something, but I was wrong.

She came to tell us that she's getting married!

'Congratulations!' Mum smiled. 'Isn't that nice?' she said, when they'd gone.

'Does that mean she's going to move?' I asked. I rather like the idea of having an empty house on both sides.

'Dougie, don't you ever listen? He is going to move into her house.'

'Oh,' I said. 'Mr and Mrs Grim.'

'I've told you not to call her that,' said Mum. I've called her Mrs Grim for so long, I have no idea what her real name is. 'And she'll take his surname when she gets married anyway. She'll be called Mrs Speck.'

'Do you think the dogs will be friends?' I asked.

'Humphrey is a guide dog,' said Mum. 'Mr Speck is blind.'

Ah, so Mr Speck is blind. That explains why he's marrying Mrs Grim.

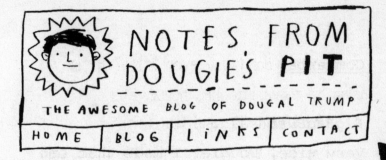

SALAD
CREAM crispe

You Will Need:

- One large packet crisps
- One small jar salad cream

Method:

Crush crisps into the salad cream, stir and eat with spoon.

119

MORE ABOUT the AUTHOR

Dougal is at present conducting an experiment in his room, to understand the mould-growing process. To this end, he has put a frankfurter under his bed, to see how much mould he can grow on it.

Comments:

BigBadBurt said:
Very nice, Dougie. I made that one
without setting fire to anything.

TrussBilly said:
Dougie, 'Crisp' doesn't have an e
on the end.

DynamoDougie said:
I know that.

TrussBilly said:
So why does it have an e in the
title of your recipe?

DynamoDougie said:
Sometimes you put an e on the

end of words to make them posh.

BigBadBurt said:
Is this a posh recipe?

DynamoDougie said:
They don't come posher.

IhateDougie said:
Hollow tree after school tomorrow.
Make sure no one sees you.

BoingBrain said:
Hello, *IhateDougie!* I haven't
seen you on here before. I'm
Claude and I'm still trying to get
the salad cream out of the bottle.

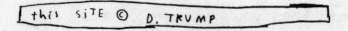

The hollow tree- again

I was very jittery at school today. I was thinking about what would happen when I put my hand in the hollow tree on the way home. Would I find Sybil in there? I'd followed the instructions — surely *IhateDougie* would give her back now?

I was also thinking about what happened to Burt. He wasn't in the hollow tree on the way to school this morning, so I do hope he is happy somewhere with lots of lovely mice to eat. Burt the bullfrog, that is, not Burt the defender. He'll be happy tucking into one of his mum's dinners. And he wouldn't fit into the hollow tree anyway.

The others thought I was jittery because of yesterday's disaster against Highton Wanderers. They couldn't talk about anything else on the way home from school, but I stayed silent, waiting for the moment I could sneak my hand into the tree.

'Why are you being so quiet, Dougie?' asked George. 'Is it because we lost the match?'

'At least we're still above Ocklesford Rovers,' said Burt.

'But we need to be careful, or Shepton Academicals will catch us up,' said Billy. 'Just as well they drew yesterday.'

We were now approaching the hollow tree and I was hanging back while the others went ahead, talking about a replacement goalie for Fairford United. They didn't notice me putting my hand in the tree.

I pulled out a small cardboard box.

Not big enough for a plate-sized tarantula.

I put my hand in again, in case Sybil was running around in there, but all I could feel were some sweet wrappers, crisp packets and old chewing gum that stuck to my fingers.

The box had a fiver taped to it, but no note.

I put the box in my bag, ran to catch the others up and told them that even the best goalies have off days and I was irreplaceable.

'We've stopped talking about that now,' said George. 'Where have you been?'

'Nowhere,' I said.

'You've been spending a lot of time in nowhere,' said Billy.

'He's been searching the hollow tree,' said Claude.

'I have not!' I said. 'I was tying up my shoelace.'

They all looked down. 'How come your shoelaces are still untied then?' asked Burt.

'They must have got undone again,' I said. I bent down to tie them up before they could say anything else.

As soon as I got home, I went straight upstairs and opened the box.

I was right – it wasn't Sybil.

This creature's only got four legs, for a start. And it isn't hairy. It's stripy and patterned. It's got five long toes on each foot with little claws. It's got big brown eyes.

126

It's cute!

I went on ZooBlog and identified my new creature as a Yucatan banded gecko. After some questions and answers with others on the blog, I knew exactly how to care for him.

I had to turn Burt's fish tank into his new home. First I tipped out the compost and replaced it with dry newspaper and gravel. I found a nice big rock for him to hide under because geckos like that. This rock had a couple of centipedes and some woodlice on it, which would do for the gecko's starters. I had to make sure it was all very dry, so I used Sibble's hairdryer to dry the gravel and rock, but not the centipedes or woodlice.

It took me a long time to pick the gravel up after I'd blown it all around my room.

I put a cricket in the gecko's tank for his main course and put him in. He went straight under the rock to hide — the gecko, I mean, not the cricket: he just hopped around with no idea he was going to be someone's dinner. Then the gecko wandered out from behind the rock and ate his cricket.

I'm glad no one has noticed that I now have a gecko living in my room. Everyone still thinks I have Sybil. Apart from my friends, who have promised to keep quiet. I hope they can — her life depends on it.

mrs GRIM AND the graveL

I've been grounded again.

It all started when I went downstairs to try out a new recipe.

'Dougie, where has all this mess come from?' Mum pointed to a very small amount of compost that I must have dropped when I was taking Burt's tank out.

'It's only a little bit of dirt,' I said. 'It could have come from anywhere.'

That's when Sibble came in. 'Mum, there's dirt all over the house! And there's a trail of it up to Dougie's room.'

Mum gave me that look that meant I'd better explain myself.

'Oh, that,' I said casually. 'I had to change the compost in Sybil's cage.'

That was enough to keep them quiet for about two seconds. Then Sibble remembered that Sybil has vermiculite, not compost.

'I couldn't find the vermiculite,' I said.

'Typical,' said Mum. 'Perhaps you should tidy your room.'

'And I can't find my hairdryer,' said Sibble. 'Someone's taken it.' She narrowed her eyes at me.

'Why are you looking at me?' I said.

'Because I could hear you using it in your room,' said Sibble.

'Dougie, give Sybil her hairdryer back,' said Mum.

'I never took it!' I yelled, in my best innocent voice.

'You so did!' screamed Sibble. 'And I don't want to use it ever again if you've touched it!'

'Oh, good, can I keep it then?' I said.

Both Mum and Sibble were about to shout, but I was saved by the doorbell. Or so I thought.

Mrs Grim was at the door, wanting to know why she'd seen me pinching gravel from her drive. 'And one of the rocks from my front border is missing.'

'I needed some gravel for school,' I said. 'For the fish tank. The rock is for the fish to swim round. I'll get a merit for it.'

Mrs Grim started to say something, but I was saved by a car pulling up outside our house, driven by none other than Mr Truss. Out climbed Billy, George, Burt and Claude.

'Very kind of you to have them all for tea,' said Mr Truss. 'Just call me if they get too much and I'll pick them up.'

Mum didn't say anything. Mrs Grim took

one look at my grinning friends and scuttled back to her house, muttering darkly about gravel and fish tanks.

'Dougie!' hissed Mum, as my friends made their way upstairs. 'Why did you invite them without telling me?'

'I didn't,' I said, as I ran upstairs after them.

'What am I going to feed them?' she said.

I stopped. 'Anything but brown goo will do nicely.'

I didn't hear her reply. My friends were now in my room and I didn't want them to see my new creature. I had to rush past them and throw a Stamford United shirt over the gecko's tank. No one seemed to notice, thank goodness.

'Now, Dougie,' said George, 'we have

all come round because you have been acting very oddly – ever since your spider disappeared.'

'She didn't disappear, I was lying,' I said, pointing at the Stamford United shirt. 'Sybil is under there having a sleep.'

They all looked at me, apart from Claude, who was busy tunnelling under my bed.

Before I could stop him, Burt lifted the Stamford United shirt. 'That is not Sybil under there. And it's not the creature I saw last time either.'

'Unless it's lost a bit of weight,' said George. 'And gone all stripy.'

'It looks like a gecko,' said Billy.

'What's it called?' asked Burt.

'Nothing,' I said.

'Well,' said George, 'I think we should call it Billy. Billy the Geeko.'

'Yeah, Billy the Geeko,' said Burt. 'But where's the bullfrog? I liked him.'

'There is no bullfrog,' I said. 'Please don't tell anyone. If you do, then Sybil will lose her legs, one by one.'

They were all silent for a while. Until Claude spoke.

'There's something horrible under the bed,' he said, coming out looking very pale. 'It looks like a giant hairy spider leg.'

For a split second there was silence. Then I explained. 'That is not a spider leg,' I said. 'Any fool can see that is my experiment to see how much mould I can grow on a frankfurter. As you can see, quite a lot. What were you doing under my bed anyway?'

'I was looking for Claude the worm.'

'Burt ate Claude the worm.' The words slipped out before I could stop them.

Burt started to say that he hadn't eaten Claude the worm, but his words were stopped by a scream from downstairs. Then another. And another. Then footsteps all the way up to my room. Mum stood at the door.

'Dougie! WHAT have you been putting in my freezer?'

Mum was holding an ice-cream container full of frozen mice.

CHOCOLATE AND MARSHMALLOW NIBBLES

You Will Need:

- One jar chocolate spread
- One packet small biscuits
- One packet small marshmallows

More ABOUT the AUTHOR

Dougal Trump's dad is always losing the TV remote. He stomps about expecting everyone else to hunt for it. He makes you get up to make sure you are not sitting on it. His catchphrase is 'Who's got the TV remote?'

137

Method:

- Open packet of biscuits and eat all the broken ones. If there aren't any broken ones, break some and eat them.
- Spread a generous amount of chocolate spread on each biscuit. This is quite fiddly and you'll have to lick your fingers a lot.
- Put one or two small marshmallows on top. Eat the remaining marshmallows.

Comments:

BigBadBurt said:
Far too fiddly! I just put it all in a big bowl, stirred it and ate it.

138

Superspeed said:
Were you allowed out of your room
to make this? I thought you were
grounded?

TrussBilly said:
Were you grounded for lying about
why you pinched Mrs Grim's gravel
(sorry I couldn't stop my dad
from saying that there is no fish
tank in our classroom), or for
keeping the mice in the freezer?

SweetAngieBabe said:
I can't believe you keep mice in your
freezer! You are even more disgusting
than I thought. Tell your sister I
got a new nail varnish — Blue Hazy
Haze — and it's really cool.

BoingBrain said:
What happened to the mice?

DynamoDougie said:
The mice are safely back in the freezer, in order to feed my tarantula, who is not missing. No more comments. Goodbye.

IhateDougie said:
You did not follow the instructions in my last note. Now, do you have a recipe for Sybil soup?

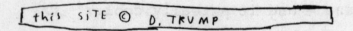

DynamoDougie said:
Don't hurt Sybil, it's not her fault! What note??

The UNFAir Grounding of the dog

I can't believe it. My cruel and heartless parents have grounded the dog.

It's Humphrey the guide dog's fault.

It all started because, while being stuck up in my room because I am now ubergrounded, I've been spying on the Grims.

Mr Grim is spending a lot of time there now. I know his name isn't really Mr Grim, but I think that name suits him, so that is what I'm going to call him.

Mr Grim is a keen gardener like Mrs Grim. I've been watching him pottering along, pruning shrubs and pulling up weeds. I saw him kneel by the pond and pull lots of stuff out of it. He then trimmed the hedge on the other side of the garden with the electric hedge trimmers. Then he used the shears to give it another snip, while Mrs Grim tidied up the mess.

As I watched him, a little suspicion entered my head.

Mum and Dad were in our garden. Mum was filling some big old pots with the compost that I'd found for Burt. She was wearing rubber gloves and trying to look like a keen gardener.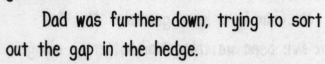

Dad was further down, trying to sort out the gap in the hedge.

The dog was somewhere in between, digging a hole by Mrs Grim's fence.

Humphrey the guide dog was on the other side of the fence, digging his way towards our dog. I wondered whether the tunnels would join up.

Mr Grim walked over to the fence and shouted at Humphrey to stop digging. He called over to Mum, who stopped filling her pots and went to talk to him. He pointed to his dog and then pointed over the fence to our dog. Mum called Dad and they both made a big fuss of getting the dog inside.

My little suspicion was growing bigger.

It's obvious that Mr Grim didn't like the dogs digging. But how did he know what they were up to when he's supposed to be blind? How could he do all that pruning and stuff? With electric hedge-trimmers?

I've decided his behaviour is most suspicious.

I asked Billy the Geeko what he thought. He gave me a couple of solemn blinks with his big eyes. I think he sort of nodded his head as well. Burt wasn't there to gulp his approval.

I miss Burt. I miss Sybil.

I took a sad look out of the window, just in time to see our dog escape from the house. He went straight back to the fence and started digging again. And he got through! The hole did join up with Humphrey's and I watched him wriggle and squirm his way to the other side. He trotted into the Grims' garden with bits of earth sticking to him, looking very pleased with himself. Then he saw something come out of the house:

Mrs Grim's precious cat called Precious.

What a silly time to come out into the garden. Our poor dog didn't know whether to play chase with Humphrey, or chase the cat.

He chose to chase the cat.

Now the dog has been grounded for teaching Humphrey the proper way to chase a cat. The Grims have accused him of being a bad influence. I would like to know what difference it makes – I don't think Mr Grim needs a guide dog at all. In fact, if my suspicions are correct, Humphrey is probably only a proper dog anyway.

I think Mr Grim is only pretending to be blind. Now, all I need is a cunning plan to prove it. And find out *why*.

A DEVIOUS PLAN

I've just thought of a devious plan, which will prove that Mr Grim is a charlatan and only pretending to be blind. I will need your help for this cunning plan and will tell you all about it at school tomorrow.

MORE ABOUT the AUTHOR

Another thing Dougal does when he's grounded, is sneak outside his loft room and listen to his sister, who likes making phone calls on the landing. Most of them are boring, but sometimes they are funny —

BLAH BLAH BLAH BLAH!

like when she talks to her friends about boys. She's been mentioning the name *Eric* a lot lately and going all giggly.

Comments:

Superspeed said:

How cunning is your cunning plan? Your last one, to put joke soap in the girls' toilets to turn their hands black, didn't really work, did it?

SweetAngieBabe said:

Was that when he had to have a big talk about why boys shouldn't go into the girls' toilets?

TrussBilly said:

I thought your last devious plan was the one where we were supposed to leave the classroom one by one to see if my dad noticed. You went first. Dad noticed. You had to stay in at break.

BigBadBurt said:

What's a charlatan?

TrussBilly said:

A charlatan is a false pretender.

BoingBrain said:

Forgot to tell you, I found a note in the hollow tree.

DynamoDougie said:

What note? What did it say?

BoingBrain said:

At the bottom it said I had to eat it.

DynamoDougie said:

What else did it say?

BoingBrain said:

I can't remember. I ate it.

*IhateDougie
said:*

DEAR DOUGIE,
PLEASE BE VERY CAREFUL.
PLEASE KEEP QUIET ABOUT
ALL THIS AND DON'T LET
YOUR SILLY FRIENDS SEE
THE NOTES FROM THE HOLLOW
TREE. I'M GETTING VERY
THIN AND MY LEGS ARE IN
DANGER. HE WILL CUT THEM
OFF AND SEND THEM TO YOU
ONE BY ONE IF YOU DON'T
DO EXACTLY AS HE SAYS.
PLEASE DELETE THE ENTRY.
YOUR LOVING SYBIL

DynamoDougie said:

My darling Sybil,

Hang on in there, girl! I am
doing all I can to keep you safe.
Unfortunately there is nothing I
can do about my friends. They knew
you were gone before he told me
not to tell — honest! I hope he is
giving you live crickets to eat
and special little mice, which are
available from all good pet shops.

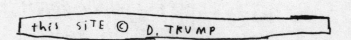

IhateDougies aid:
Go to the hollow tree. NOW.
Or else. Bring Billy. The
gecko, not the geek.

Another horrible, awful and terrible thing has happened

I sat looking at the last comment from *IhateDougie* for a long time before I deleted it. Then I got Billy the Geeko ready for his journey. I put my hand in the fish tank and this time he came right over to it – he's getting used to me now. It was easy to cup my hands over him and lift him out, with only a bit of his tail sticking out through my fingers. I put him back into the box he came in, which I lined with kitchen paper. He gave me one last blink before I put the lid on.

I'm going to miss Billy the Geeko.

I could hear Sibble on the landing, moaning on her mobile. No way could I get past her without her telling Mum or Dad that I was sneaking out. So I just had to wait at the top of my spiral stairs and listen.

'But I told you,' I heard her moan, 'I haven't got any money, so I can't come to the cinema with you. Anyway, if you're my boyfriend, you should pay.'

Boyfriend?

A great big grin went across my face. For two reasons. One, because Sibble's got a boyfriend. And two, because I now had a plan.

I took one of the fivers that I found in the hollow tree and waved it in front of Sibble's face.

'Oh, poo, my brother's being annoying again, I've got to go. Bye, Eric.' She finished the call. 'What are you doing, you annoying little twerp?'

'Was that Angela's brother, Eric?' I asked. 'Is he your boyfriend?'

'None of your business!'

'Would you like a fiver to go to the cinema with him?' I dangled it in front of her face.

She tried to snatch it away, but I was too fast for her.

'You can have it if you don't say anything when I sneak out of the house,' I said.

She looked at the five-pound note for a long time, before very slowly

taking it out of my hand. Her nails were bright blue.

'Is that Blue Hazy Haze?' I asked. But she'd already slammed her door.

I sneaked downstairs. I'd just about reached the front door when the stupid dog saw me. He started barking and wagging his tail, like he does when he thinks you're about to take him for a walk.

'Hurry up and take that dog out, so I can hear the TV!' Dad called out from the living room.

Result!

'Just don't let him in the river,' Mum called from the living room.

The dog pulled me all the way to the fields. I let him off as soon as we were through the gate, or else I think my arms would have come off. I went straight to the hollow tree.

There was something in there. It was long, thin, very light and wrapped in kitchen paper. I put it in my pocket and carefully placed Billy the Geeko in the hollow tree. I hope he's all right.

I was about to unwrap the kitchen paper parcel, when I heard a splash. Followed by excited yaps and more splashes.

The dog was in the river.

The River Ockle is really a big stream, with just enough water for a dog who's determined to get wet. And muddy. The dog took no notice of my shouting, so I had to slither down and haul him out.

I told him what I thought of him all the way home. 'You are a stupid, wet, smelly dog and I'm going to be in so much trouble, especially as Mum asked me to . . .'

I stopped. Mum and Dad must have thought I was Sibble. And that meant . . .

My foot caught something on the pavement in front of Mrs Grim's house. I tripped and landed flat on my face. The dog thought it was great. He thought I'd fallen over just so he could leap all over me and lick my face.

'Geroff!' I shouted.

'I'm terribly sorry.' Mr Grim was standing over me, holding a pair of shears. 'I must have left these on the pavement after I'd trimmed the hedge. Are you all right?'

'I'm fine,' I said, as I tried to untangle myself from the dog.

As I watched him go back inside, I was thinking. If Mr Grim is supposed to be blind, how come he can trim a hedge and then come rushing out when I tripped over his

158

shears? I decided I would have to bring my cunning plan forward.

Just as soon as I knew what my cunning plan was.

In the meantime, I had to sneak inside with the wet and smelly dog, then sneak upstairs. I'd gone up about three steps when I heard a noise coming from the living room. A sort of squealing, shouting noise that meant the dog had decided to say hello to Mum and Dad. The sort of waggy-tail, climb-all-over-you greeting. The sort that had Mum and Dad abandoning their quiet evening in front of the TV to come out and yell about what did they tell you about not letting the dog in the river?

To Sibble.

'What?' Sibble stomped out of her room. 'I never took the dog out! It was . . .' I could tell she was about to point her Blue Hazy Hazed finger at me. Then she must have remembered the fiver. And the mealworms. 'Well – sorreee.' She pouted, then slammed her door.

They didn't ground her or anything. They just looked at me and asked how I'd managed to get covered in mud when I was supposed to be grounded in my room.

'I was cleaning out Sybil's tank,' I said. 'You can come and look if you like.'

Mum decided not to. Dad said he'd see if he could try and watch five minutes of TV in peace. I went up to my room.

I carefully took the kitchen paper out of my pocket. If it was another creature in there, I hoped it was all right. But I couldn't really think of a creature that would be that shape. Maybe it was a fiver.

160

It wasn't a fiver. It was something very, very horrible.

It was a dried up, very hairy, very large spider leg. It came with a note:

DON'T LET YOUR FRIENDS SEE ANY MORE OF MY NOTES. TELL THEM YOUR SPIDER IS SAFE AND YOU ARE A BIG LIAR, OR ELSE YOU WILL RECEIVE ANOTHER LEG.

SYBIL IS SAFE AND SOUND AND I AM A BIG LIAR

There, I've said it.

more ABOUT the AUTHOR

Dougal Trump is a liar.

Comments:

SweetAngieBabe said:
Well — DUH!

Superspeed said:
I don't believe you. I think you are lying about being a liar.

TrussBilly said:

Were you lying when you told Dad
the dog ate your homework?

BigBadBurt said:

Can you post another recipe?

BoingBrain said:

When you said that you could save
two penalties at once — that wasn't
a lie, was it?

IhateDougie said:

Hollow tree after school
tomorrow — or else.

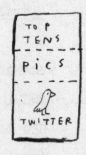

ANother New CREATURE

Last night I spent some time on ZooBlog to see how easily a bird-eating spider can manage on seven legs. They do lose legs sometimes, but they grow them back. That's because, like all spiders, giant bird-eaters moult. That means, every now and again, they get too big for their skin and it splits open. Then, out comes a brand-new and slightly bigger spider!

Mum's always finding shrivelled-up spider skins. She thinks they're dead spiders – what she doesn't know is that it's just an old skin and there will be a new spider nearby. These skins are great for scaring big sisters with.

AHHHH!

Imagine what would happen if humans moulted like spiders? We'd see shrivelled-up human skins lying around and mums would never stop complaining about the mess.

This morning I checked the hollow tree on the way to school, but there was nothing in it. I also asked Claude if he'd taken anything out of it, just in case. Then I asked the others. They all promised they'd never taken anything out of the tree.

'We leave all the notes and stuff in there for you,' said George. 'To make sure nothing happens to Sybil.'

'Sybil is fine,' I lied.

They all went quiet. I wish I could tell them the truth. But I can't risk poor Sybil losing any more legs.

At school I pretended everything was fine. I made my usual amount of noise and

166

had to stay in at break. I think Mr Truss
was relieved that I was behaving normally
again. On the way back from school, I
distracted everyone by asking them to guess
what my devious plan for Mr Grim was. (I was
hoping that someone would guess something
that I could actually use.)

This is what they came up with:

George – stand in front of Mr Grim and
    make a funny face.
Burt – sneak up behind him and yell *Boo!*
Billy – ask him how he lost his sight and
    then verify the facts on the internet.
Claude – give him three pieces of fruit
    and ask him to peel them.

My friends aren't very good at devious plans.
But it kept them from noticing that I'd stuck

my hand in the hollow tree and brought out
a small box, which was now in my school bag
making an odd noise.

'What's that noise?' asked Burt.

'Nothing,' I said, to hide the sound of
scratching.

'Do you mean the
scratching noise coming
from Dougie's bag?'
asked Claude.

I coughed. 'That
was me, coughing.'
I coughed again. 'I'd
better run home before I give you all a
bad cough.'

By the time I'd run home, I was coughing
for real.

After a bit of puffing and panting to
get my breath back, I went upstairs to see

what was in the box. I opened it carefully.
There was a small clear container inside. I
stared at what was in there for a long time,
while my mouth went

It's big, black and shiny, has eight legs
(one more than poor Sybil), two great big
claws at the front and a giant sting at the
back.

It's the biggest, coolest scorpion I've
ever seen.

I went on to ZooBlog and found out that my latest creature is an Emperor scorpion. They are the largest type of scorpion, but they aren't as dangerous as they look. If they sting you, it's no worse than a bee. They eat crickets and mealworms. I've got enough crickets but I might have to buy some more mealworms.

I washed the fish tank again and put a thick layer of Sybil's vermiculite in it, mixed with Mum's garden compost. Then I washed Billy the Geeko's rock and found another plant pot, as scorpions also like to hide when they're not scuttling about. I soaked some cotton wool in water and put that in a saucer for him to drink from. Scorpions don't like direct light, so I put a school shirt over the top of the tank and used Sybil's lamp to keep him warm.

Using the big tweezers Mr Wellington
gave me, I carefully picked him up by his
sting and gently lowered him into the tank.
He had a little run around and then I used
the tweezers to give him a cricket. I
watched him munching away, then I gave
him a mealworm for pudding. After that he
went behind his rock. I was glad he'd settled
in so quickly.

I went downstairs to see what delightful
recipe I could make for myself. But as I went
past the living room, I could see Mum outside.
She was talking to Mr Grim, who was in his
front garden with Humphrey. Humphrey had his
guide-dog harness on.

I went outside.

'Are you about to go somewhere with
Humphrey?' I asked.

'Don't interrupt,' said Mum.

'Oh, that's all right,' said Mr Grim. I couldn't see if he was looking right at me, because he had his sunglasses on. 'Yes, I'm taking Humphrey to the fields for a bit of a run.'

'But how will you manage when you let him off the lead?' asked Mum.

'Oh, he doesn't go far,' said Mr Grim.

Mum rubbed her chin, which she does when she's thinking. 'Why don't you take Dougie and our dog with you?'

I had several excuses ready:

EXCUSES LIST:

- TOO MUCH HOMEWORK
- I WAS SUPPOSED to BE GROUNDED
- The Dog would pull Me Over
- the dog would teach Humphrey BAD Habits
- mum would miss me too much
- We hardly KNEW Mr GRIM
- he was ONLY pretending to Be Blind aNd MY Life might Be IN Danger

But I kept quiet.

That's because I had a cunning plan forming in my mind.

'OK,' I said. 'I'll go and get the dog.'

NOTES FROM DOUGIE'S PIT

A Message to my Followers

This is to let all my followers know that I am ubergrounded. I don't think I'm ever going to be let out of this room again.

Please tell Tom

More ABOUT the AUTHOR

Sometimes Dougal gets grounded for something that was sort of his fault. Like what happened when he tried to prove that Mr Grim isn't really blind.

UBERGROUNDED

that I will still practise my
goal-keeping skills, as I know I
have a ball in my room somewhere.
And ask him to persuade my dad
to let me out for matches. And
training. And tactics talks at
George's house.

If that doesn't work, I'm thinking
of packing a bag and escaping.
George, can I come and live with
you? I'm sure your mum won't notice
one extra.

Comments:

Superspeed said:
We can always put Billy in goal.
Or Burt. You can live here if you

want, but don't pinch my trainers
if you lose yours.

SweetAngieBabe said:
'Followers'? Since when did you
have followers?

TrussBilly said:
Weren't you already ubergrounded?
Technically, you are now uber-
ubergrounded.

BigBadBurt said:
Can we have another recipe?

Boingbrain said:
Why are you grounded? Are you going
to tell us your cunning plan?

DynamoDougie said:

It was my cunning plan that got me grounded.

IhateDougie said:

I don't care how grounded you are. You will bring the giant scorpion back when I ask. Or you will find another of Sybil's legs in the hollow tree.

178

MY <u>CUNNING</u> <u>PLAN</u> AND HOW it WENT WRONG

This was my cunning plan:

BING!

CUNNING PLAN

* Go off to the fields with the dog, Mr Grim and Humphrey.
* Let our dogs off the lead.
* Ask Mr Grim if I could look at Humphrey's guide-dog harness.
* Put Humphrey's harness on our dog.
* If Mr Grim notices that the harness is on the wrong dog, then he can't be blind.

Simple, yet brilliant. What could possibly go wrong?

When we arrived at the fields, I freed the dog and he shot off like a cannon. Mr Grim carefully took Humphrey's harness off and Humphrey bounded after our dog. I had no idea Humphrey could run so fast.

Mr Grim and I walked to the river – we could hear the dogs splashing about long before we got there. Mr Grim had a small white stick which he waved in front of him. I don't know how it was supposed to help him – he wasn't even touching the ground with it.

'This is so people know I can't see well,' he said. 'But as long as I can hear you next to me, I know where I'm going.'

I nearly believed him. But then we reached the river. 'They're having a good time in there, aren't they?' said Mr Grim, watching the two dogs.

I repeat: *watching* the two dogs. Even with his sunglasses on, I could see he was looking right at them.

Time to put my plan into action.

'How come Humphrey doesn't pull you along like my dog?' I asked.

'He's well trained,' said Mr Grim. 'He was training right from when he was a little puppy. When he was nearly two years old, I started to train with him. I spent a month learning how to handle him and then he became my guide dog. He's changed my life, has Humphrey.' He turned to me as he said this. 'I'm very lucky.'

He sounded very convincing. I was about

to ask him whether he was an actor, but I remembered to stick to the plan.

'Is it easy to put the harness on?' I asked.

'Oh yes,' said Mr Grim, showing me. 'You do it like this.' When he'd finished, I asked him, in as innocent a way as I could, if I could put it on Humphrey for him.

'Of course you can,' he said.

The dogs were having a great time in the river, but Humphrey came out when Mr Grim called him and our dog followed.

It was quite a struggle getting the harness on our dog. He wouldn't stop wriggling, because he didn't like the harness and because Humphrey had decided to go back in the river. By the time the dog had the harness on, I was soaking wet.

It was a struggle to hand the harness

to Mr Grim, but I managed. I'm not a local hero for nothing.

I'm not any sort of hero now.

Mr Grim took hold of the harness at the exact moment the dog decided to follow Humphrey back into the river. At top speed.

With Mr Grim holding on for dear life.

Mr Grim ended up sitting in the river with the two dogs.

I ended up sitting in the river next to Mr Grim, trying to explain myself.

'I was trying to see if you really were blind,' I said.

Mr Grim then did something very surprising. He laughed. A lot. With his head back and everything. So much that the dogs stopped mucking about and stood there looking at him. 'Well, I'm glad I've learned to manage so well,' he said, when he'd finally finished.

Then he explained how he does it. He only has to go somewhere a couple of times to get a picture in his head. Then his feet remember where to go. That's why he can wander around Mrs Grim's garden like a seeing person.

He can also hear very well. And his sense of smell is very good.

'I wondered why you put the harness on the wrong dog,' he said, as he sat in the river with me.

'How did you know it was the wrong dog?'

'He sounds different. He moans a lot, doesn't he? I could tell that he didn't think much of Humphrey's harness.'

'But why did you take the handle?' I asked.

Mr Grim just laughed. 'I was going to pretend that I hadn't noticed,' he said. 'I was curious to see what you'd do next.'

What I did next was rush into the river, trying to stop Mr Grim from falling over and breaking his arm.

And that is why I am uber-ubergrounded. Mum and Dad couldn't stop apologizing to Mr Grim. They said they didn't know what to do with me, they really didn't.

Mr Grim just laughed and said we were all young once. He said that I should take Humphrey for a walk with our dog more often. Then he asked me how you can tell if you've broken your arm.

I think I like Mr Grim.

He's given me a great idea. I now have a cunning plan to catch *IhateDougie* and get Sybil back.

STAN WITZEL
AND the
MEALWORMS

Being uber-ubergrounded is boring. I'm only
allowed out to go to the toilet and to go to
school. Both are about as exciting as each
other.

But today in school I did have a bit of
excitement.

We went on a school trip. When I
say 'school trip', it was only a walk down
Ocklesford High Street. We were supposed to
be learning about shops. I have absolutely no
idea what we were supposed be learning about
them, but it was better than being in the
classroom.

We walked past Ocklesford Pet Shop. It
had a big notice in the window:

187

NEW!
EXOTIC PETS
NOW IN STORE.
INCLUDING SOME
RARE SPECIES.

- - - - - - - - - -
VIVARIUMS, tANKS,
SUBSTRATE AVAILABLE
- - - - - - - - - -
LIVE MEALWORMS
SOLD HERE

I waited until Mr Truss, his assistant and the parent helpers weren't looking, then swung open the pet-shop door and nipped inside.

Only to bump into someone hurrying out of the shop.

It was none other than Stan Witzel.

Stan who wouldn't know one end of a pet from another. He must have gone into the wrong shop. He rushed past me, banging me with his rucksack, and slammed the door behind him.

I wandered up to the counter. The owner, Mr Biscuit, was on the phone. I know Mr Biscuit because he sold my hamster to me. He is also responsible for suggesting that my parents rescue a dog. Unfortunately, I think we rescued the wrong dog.

I stood by the counter, listening to the phone call.

'Hello, Mr Conti, Mr Biscuit from Ocklesford Pet Shop here. Your rare Savu python is ready for collection. She's in a box and will be happy there until you come for her . . . Yes, her name is Freda. She's very well, it's just that her previous owner fell out of a tree and can't look after her any more. Bye now.' He put the phone down and looked at me. 'Yes, young man, what can I do for you?'

'I'd like some mealworms.'

'How many?'

I did a quick calculation in my head. 'A hundred and sixty.'

'They come in boxes,' said Mr Biscuit. 'Small, medium or large.' He went over to a shelf, which had clear plastic boxes on it. 'And what size mealworm do you want?'

'I'll have five pounds' worth of the big ones.' I pulled out the last fiver from *IhateDougie*.

Mr Biscuit lifted one of the lids and revealed an amazing sight. Thousands of mealworms wriggling about like giant vegetarian maggots. Then he put his hand in and filled up a couple of containers for

me. It was great.
I helped him.
Mealworms are
very wriggly.

'You're not
going to let these
loose in the classroom, are you?' he asked,
as I stuffed the containers in my pockets.

'No,' I said. 'I'm going to feed them to
my sco—' I nearly said *scorpion*, but managed
to stop myself in time. 'They're for my
crickets. Who I feed to my tarantula.'

'You have a tarantula? Where did you
get it from?'

'Mr Wellington at the London Zoological
Association. I'm looking after her until she
finds a home.'

'Ah,' said Mr Biscuit. 'Mr Wellington is a
good friend of mine. He's been a great help

in setting me up to sell exotic pets.'

'Can I see your exotic pets?'

'Of course. I've just boxed a Savu python for a new customer. Would you like to see her? I put her on the end of the counter, just . . .' He stared at the counter. 'She's gone,' he said. 'The Savu python has gone, box and all. She was here on the counter just before you came in.'

I knew how he felt. That's exactly how I lost my poor Sybil.

MEALWORM HYSTERICS

You Will Need:

- Two small boxes of wriggly mealworms
- One classroom full of kids (including lots of girls)
- One boring teacher

Method:

Open the boxes and wait . . .

Comments:

Superspeed said:
That was great! I haven't laughed
so much since you brought that slug
to school and said it was your pet.
How many break-times do you have to
stay in for now?

TrussBilly said:
I think the girls screamed because
you hid the boxes of mealworms in
your lunchbox.

BigBadBurt said:
Did you mean to open the box of
mealworms, or did you think your
sandwiches were in it?

BoingBrain said:

Mum found a mealworm in my collar.

She's still screaming.

SweetAngieBabe said:

Dougal Trump, you are disgusting.

You are so not coming to my party.

DynamoDougie said:

What party?

Superspeed said:

The one you're not invited to.

You're ubergrounded anyway.

TrussBilly said:

Uber-ubergrounded.

IhateDougie said:

If you want Sybil to keep her legs,
get to the usual place. NOW! Bring
the you-know-what.

ANOTHER CUNNING PLAN

It's a shame I had to take the scorpion back so soon. Of all my creatures, I think he settled in the quickest and was happy to scuttle around in his tank. I wish I could have got to know him better. I hadn't even given him a name.

The thing about Emperor scorpions is that, as long as you are very careful and they think your hand is just another piece of wood or stone, you can let them crawl on you. So I put my hand into the fish tank

and waited. Eventually he clambered on to my hand. I waited again, then gently lifted him out. He seemed quite happy to crawl over my hand, so I thought I'd let him have a little runabout before I put him in the box. He was halfway up my arm when Mum came in with my clean laundry.

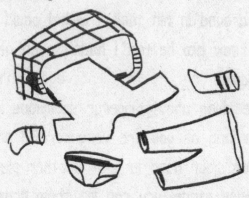

She opened her mouth. She dropped the laundry. She went back out again. Without closing her mouth. Without making a sound. I didn't hear the scream until the scorpion was safely in his box.

I went downstairs and found Mum staring at a pile of onions, which were about to suffer the horrible fate of going in her brown goo.

'Mum?'

She jumped.

'I'm going to take Humphrey out for a walk now,' I said. 'OK?'

She nodded.

I'd just reached the front door when she called me.

'Dougie?'

'Yeah?'

'When I went into your room just now, what exactly was that on your arm?'

'Just a scorpion. Bye.'

Sometimes with Mum, it's best to pretend everything is normal. She nodded and off I went. She had no idea I had the scorpion in my bag. Or Sibble's sunglasses. Or an old cloak from the dressing-up drawer.

She had no idea that I was about to put the most cunning plan ever into action.

I went to collect Humphrey from next door. Mr Grim answered, with his arm in a sling.

'What happened to your arm?' I asked.

'I broke it when I fell in the river,' he said. But he didn't sound cross. 'I'm glad you're in one piece though, as it means you can walk Humphrey for me.' He handed me Humphrey's lead. At that moment, Mrs Grim called out something and, while Mr Grim turned to answer her, I grabbed Humphrey's harness from the hook.

Mr Grim didn't notice.

My cunning plan was going to plan.

As soon as I got to the end of the

road, I put the harness on Humphrey. I took
Sibble's sunglasses out of my pocket and put
them on. I took the cloak out of my bag
and put that on too. Then I took hold of
Humphrey's harness and stuck my head in
the air.

Disguise complete. A blind man walking
his dog. A blind man who would wander past
the hollow tree and just happen to put a
scorpion in it. A blind man who would wait and
see who took the scorpion out, without them
realizing he could see them.

I was about to look each way a hundred
times before crossing the road when a car
stopped for me. Humphrey shot across and
I had to run to keep up with him. I tripped
over the curb and nearly went flying.

He headed straight for the river and
I had to hold his harness with both hands.

It was like waterskiing on grass, with a dog instead of a boat.

Humphrey didn't stop until we were in the river.

'Hey, are you all right?' I heard a shout. I thought it sounded familiar, but it was hard to see with a dog splashing water all over Sibble's sunglasses.

So I took them off. And looked right at the man now scrabbling down the bank to help me. He stopped scrabbling down the bank and looked right back at me. Then he lost his balance and ended up sitting in the river next to me. It was Lysander Witzel.

'Hello, Mr Witzel,' I said. 'Shouldn't you be in prison?'

I have never got out of a river so fast. Luckily, Humphrey came with me. I think he thought we were playing chase. I let him chase me all the way to the hollow tree and then we hid behind it.

I watched Mr Witzel climb out of the river. I don't think he had any broken limbs. He brushed himself down and walked over the fields and out of the entrance. A few seconds later I saw his silver car speeding along the road.

He'd completely ruined my cunning plan.

I took the harness off Humphrey and put him on the lead. I made him sit while I carefully pulled the box with the scorpion out of my backpack. I hope he was all right in there after his shaky journey.

I tried to put him in the hollow tree, but there was already a box in there. A big, flat box. With a fiver taped to the top of it. And a note which said *THIS WAY UP*.

I swapped boxes. Keeping the new box

the right way up meant it only just fitted in my backpack.

I took Humphrey back. Mrs Grim opened the door.

'What do you think you're doing with Humphrey's harness?' she yelled. 'And why is it soaking wet?'

I can't believe it. Mrs Grim had been going to clean Humphrey's harness while I was out with him. She said she was coming straight round to complain, as soon as she'd put her shoes on, which gave me hardly any time to think of an excuse.

In any case, something far worse happened.

THE HUGEST
TROUBLE EVER

I think I know who *IhateDougie* is. But I can't do anything about it because I don't want to put dear Sybil at risk.

It all started when I got home. Mum and Dad were sitting in the living room, reading the *Ocklesford Gazette*.

OCKLESFORD GAZETTE

MISSING ANIMALS!

'Listen to this,' I heard Dad say. 'Poor Mr Biscuit has had some creatures stolen from his shop. He's lost an African bullfrog, a Yucatan banded gecko and an Emperor scorpion. Who would want to steal those?'

'Talking of scorpions,' said Mum. 'I'm sure I saw Dougie—'

I rushed into the living room and grabbed the paper.

'Dougie, what are you doing?' protested Mum. It was a good question. I never read the paper. And snatching the paper off my dad is a dangerous thing to do. But I had to stop them talking about the article.

Before Dad could say anything, the doorbell went *clunk*. Mrs Grim had put on her shoes and stormed round to ask why I'd taken Humphrey's harness and let him go in the river with it.

'I don't know why he took it,' she said. 'Dougal should know that guide dogs only work for their owners.' She glared at me.

'Dougie?' said Mum.

'Dougal!' said Dad.

'What's he done now?' Sibble called from upstairs. She'd come out especially to listen to me being told off.

I decided to ground myself. I went straight to my room and left Mum and Dad talking to Mrs Grim about what to do with me. I took the *Ocklesford Gazette* with me.

As soon as I'd closed the door, I had a look at the article Dad had been reading.

EXOTIC CREATURES STOLEN!

A NUMBER OF EXOTIC ANIMALS HAVE BEEN STOLEN FROM OCKLESFORD PET SHOP. THESE INCLUDE A GIANT AFRICAN BULLFROG, A YUCATAN BANDED GECKO AND AN EMPEROR SCORPION.

'THESE CREATURES NEED SPECIAL CARE,' SAID MR BISCUIT, THE SHOP'S OWNER. 'I HOPE WHOEVER HAS TAKEN THEM KNOWS HOW TO LOOK AFTER THEM.'

MR BISCUIT, SHOP OWNER

THE LATEST ANIMAL TO BE STOLEN IS A SAVU PYTHON. 'I HAD JUST GOT FREDA READY TO GO TO HER NEW OWNER,' SAID MR BISCUIT. 'AND THEN SHE WAS GONE.'
THE POLICE WOULD LIKE TO TALK TO THE CHEEKY SCHOOLBOY WHO CAME IN TO BUY MEALWORMS AT THE SAME TIME THE SAVU PYTHON WAS STOLEN.

I read the article twice to make sure. Then
I very slowly took the box out of my
backpack. I had a horrible feeling I knew
what was in it.

I was right.

I went on ZooBlog just to make sure.

It's a Savu python.

It doesn't matter how much I look
at her, she is definitely a Savu python.
It doesn't matter how much I try to
kid myself that she wasn't stolen from
Ocklesford Pet Shop, her box has got
Mr Conti written on it.

It doesn't matter how much I try to
kid myself that Mr Conti is her name. She
is a girl python, and I heard Mr Biscuit
talking to Mr Conti on the phone –
telling him his Savu python was ready for
collection.

I know her name
is Freda. I know who
stole her, but I can't
do anything about it.
Because he's got Sybil.

FREDA

NOTES FROM DOUGIE'S PIT

THE AWESOME BLOG OF DOUGAL TRUMP

| HOME | BLOG | LINKS | CONTACT |

THE IMAGININGS OF DOUGAL TRUMP

I am always imagining things. A while ago I imagined what I would do if my tarantula went missing. I even wrote on this blog about it. She isn't missing at all.

MORE ABOUT the AUTHOR

Dougal Trump has a very active imagination. He is always imagining things. Take no notice.

I never had an African bullfrog called Burt either. Nor a gecko

211

called Billy. Nor any other creature. If you see something that looks like a python in my bedroom, it's probably because you have something in your eye.

Comments:

Superspeed said:
What are you talking about? Are you going to Angela's party?

TrussBilly said:
Dougie can't come because he isn't invited.

BoingBrain said:
I've just been to Angela's party, but got the wrong house. I went

to a party for three-year-olds
instead. It was fun.

BigBadBurt said:
Angela's party was all right until
Stan Witzel turned up and put that
horrible music on. Why didn't
you stop him, Angela? Why did you
invite him anyway?

SweetAngieBabe said:
None of your business. Go away, all
of you.

DynamoDougie said:
What's wrong, Angela?

SweetAngieBabe said:
Nothing. Go away. OK, you can come

home with me tomorrow and I'll tell
you. Don't tell anyone. Delete this
message.

IhateDougie said:
Go straight home after school
tomorrow. Do not pass anyone's
house. Pass the hollow tree. Or you
will get another leg.

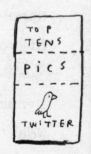

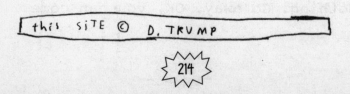

me and Angela —
UNBelievABlE!

I had a terrible dilemma. Angela Sweeter
wanted me to go home with her. *IhateDougie*
said I had to go straight home past the
hollow tree. How could I tell Angela that if I
didn't go straight home after school, my dear
Sybil would lose another leg?

Then I had a brilliant, amazing idea. All
it took was a quick word with Claude on the
way to school. It's easy to hang back and
talk to him because he often walks behind us,
dawdling along with his head in the clouds.

'Hey, Claude,' I
said. 'Would you like
to earn a fiver?' I
said it a few times
before he realized

I was talking to him. Then I repeated my instructions a couple of times to make sure. 'Just hang back on the fields on the way home and, when no one's looking, stick your hand in the hollow tree. Take whatever is in there, and hide it until I come to your house to collect it. OK?'

'You mean like you do on the way home from school every day?'

'You're not supposed to notice,' I said.

'Don't worry, we all know not to look. Do you want me to do this so you can go home with Angela?' he said. Sometimes he surprises me, does Claude.

I'd hardly got in the school gate when Angela came up to me and whispered in my ear, 'Don't tell anyone you're coming home with me, right?'

'Of course not,' I said.

By the time we went home, Claude had told everyone.

'I told you to keep it to yourself,' hissed Angela as she stomped home, with me trailing after her and her friends all giggling behind me.

'It wasn't my fault,' I said. 'Claude told everyone.'

'Who told Claude, then?'

'Why don't you want anyone to know?'

'Because,' she said, 'I don't want my boyfriend to know. OK?'

I didn't know how to reply to that one. I was still two steps behind her when we reached her house, but her friends had gone.

We went upstairs. Her bedroom is nearly as messy as mine. Except mine doesn't have bottles of nail varnish everywhere. Or skirts. Or pink socks.

'Right,' said Angela. 'You see that pile of clothes?' She pointed to a pile of stuff on a chair. 'I'm going to go out of my room and I want you to look underneath. Then I want you take what you find there and get out of my house as fast as you can.'

'Why, what's under here?' I walked over to the pile of clothes.

'No!' squeaked Angela. 'Not until I'm out of the room. Then get that thing out of there.' She shut the door and left me on my own.

I pulled the clothes off the chair. She's got even more T-shirts than my sister. But I soon forgot about that when I saw what was hidden under the pile. I couldn't believe it.

A large perspex tank. With a thick layer of vermiculite on the bottom. A large plant pot on its side, half buried in the vermiculite,

with a layer of silvery web over it. A bit
of red paint on one corner, which could only
have come from the bonnet of Dad's car.

Sybil's tank!

My smile reached from ear to ear. Then
it disappeared again. There was something in
the corner of the cage, half buried.

A dead Sybil.

All shrivelled up. All starved to death.
Poor, poor Sybil.

I wiped away a tear and lifted the lid
off the tank. I was just picking her up when

the silvery web over the plant pot quivered. I thought it was just the breeze blowing her old web, but then it quivered a bit more.

Two very large, very hairy legs appeared. Then two more. And then my darling Sybil came out, looking more beautiful than ever.

Sybil had a new coat! Even better, she had all her eight legs!

The thing in the corner of the cage was just Sybil's old skin. She must have moulted while she was away.

Sybil ran straight on to my hand. She was obviously pleased to see me.

I lifted her gently out of the tank. 'Hello, Sybil,' I said. She quivered her pincers.

'I'm very glad to see you again, but what on earth are you doing at Angela's?'

That was when Angela came back into the room. I think Sybil got a bit of a fright when Angela screamed and slammed the door, because she ran up my arm and tried to hide in my neck.

I had to keep very calm until Sybil felt better. Then I got her to climb on to my other hand and put her carefully back in her cage. I took her old skin out. I counted its legs, just to make sure.

Seven.

I put it in my bag. Then I opened Angela's door to tell her it was safe to come in now.

'Where did you get her?' I asked.

'My boyfriend gave her to me. It was supposed to be my birthday present.'

'Who is your boyfriend?'

'Well, he's not my boyfriend any more. I didn't like him anyway.'

'I should hope not,' I said.

Because despite my question, I knew exactly who her boyfriend was.

THE AMAZING things that HAPPENED AT MY HOUSE

Dad turned up at Angela's house all full of smiles, because he thought he was coming round to talk about cleaning their windows. But Angela's mum told him he'd come round to take me home because I made her darling daughter scream.

'I want that thing out of my house now,' said Angela.

Dad drove me home in a huff. 'Why did you tell Angela to tell me they wanted me to do their windows?' he moaned. 'I've a good mind to ground you for even longer. How long are you grounded for anyway?'

'I've no idea.' I smiled. I didn't care if I was grounded forever – I had Sybil's tank on my lap and that was all that mattered.

'And what were you doing with that spider at Angela's anyway?' he asked.

'She didn't believe I had a giant tarantula,' I said.

'So you showed her?' Dad grinned. 'That'll teach them to get someone else to clean their windows.'

I took Sybil straight upstairs. I gave her the mouse that I'd defrosted for the Savu python and she was very pleased with it. I dangled it over the end of her burrow, until she leaped out and grabbed it. Then I left her in peace to eat it, while I had a look at the python.

I know it's the one that was stolen from Mr Biscuit, and suppose it ought to go back to its proper owner. But I thought I'd have some fun with her first.

She's a young adult and a bit longer than my arm. She's a beautiful golden brown with darker brown markings on top and pale cream underneath. She's very friendly and likes wrapping herself round my arm. Sometimes she squeezes like she's hugging me. Mr Conti is very lucky.

I was stroking her head when I heard voices downstairs. Then footsteps all the way to my room. Mum came in.

'Dougie!' She really ought to stop coming into my room without knocking. 'Your friends have turned up again and you know you're . . . ?' She stared at my arm, which had a python slithering round it.

'Just send them up, Mum,' I said. 'Thanks.'

She was too speechless to object.

George, Billy, Claude and Burt came into my room. When they saw me with Freda, they all stopped dead, just like Mum, but without the gulps.

'Say hello to Freda,' I said.

'Cool snake,' said George.

'Will it crush you to death?' said Burt. 'Is it poisonous?'

'Hello, Freda,' said Claude.

'It's a Savu python, isn't it?' said Billy. 'They are the smallest of the pythons and like being handled. They come from—'

'Shut up, Billy!' we all said.

'Is that Sybil's cage back under your dormer window?' asked Burt.

'Yeah,' I said. 'Would you like to see her eating a mouse?' They crowded round to have a look through the back of her cage, where she was very happy with her legs all round the mouse.

'Don't disturb her,' I whispered. 'Just look.'

'Awesome,' said George.

'Is she friends with the snake?' asked Burt.

'No,' I said. 'They'd try to eat each other.'

'And what about your hamster?' asked Claude.

'Both of them would try to eat my hamster,' I said, 'so I have to keep them apart.' It was good to tell my friends about my creatures at last. Then Billy asked the question that they all obviously wanted to ask.

'Is that the stolen python?'

ThE PythoN, thE HOLLOW tREE AND mY CuNNiNg PLAN

I told them everything. All about the notes, the creatures, how I got Sybil back, the article in the *Gazette* and how I asked Claude to look in the hollow tree after school.

'What did you find in there?' I asked.

'A note,' said Claude.

'What did it say?'

'I can't remember. I ate it.'

'But we all read it first,' said George.

'And it said you had to go to the hollow tree at 6 p.m. this evening and bring the you-know-what,' said Burt.

'What's a you-know-what?' asked Claude.

'The Savu python,' we all replied at once.

'So what do we do now?' asked George.

'We carry out my cunning plan,' I said.

They all groaned.

At exactly ten minutes to six, we left the house. We walked out in a bunch, so Mum didn't realize I was in the middle and sneaking out even though I'm grounded.

Then we sneaked away and carried on sneaking, until we realized we'd look less suspicious if we weren't sneaking.

We walked on to the fields and played some football. Then, at precisely six o'clock, I went to the hollow tree and put the box Freda came in back in there. But Freda wasn't in the box, she was happy back home in the fish tank.

Once the box was in the tree, we pretended to go home. But we crept back and hid in the long grass and undergrowth by the river near the hollow tree.

230

We didn't have to wait long. Soon a man came along. He was wearing an old-fashioned tweed jacket, sunglasses and a baseball cap. He had an enormous moustache. He stuck his hand in the hollow tree and took out the box. 'Got you!' he said. His voice was very familiar. I couldn't believe it. It was the last person I expected.

Mr Wellington from the Zoological Association.

That was the moment Claude slipped down the bank into the river. But before he went, he grabbed on to Billy. When Billy started slipping, he grabbed on to George, who grabbed on to Burt, who grabbed on to me, so we all went sliding into the river like dominoes.

Dominoes making a lot of noise.

'Oh dear,' said Mr Wellington, looking down

at the five of us sitting in the river. 'Dougal, why did you put this box in the hollow tree just now?'

We all scrambled up.

I looked at Mr Wellington. 'I wanted to catch the person who's been stealing creatures from Mr Biscuit,' I said.

'Ah,' he said. 'So did I.' And then he told us why he'd come to the hollow tree. 'The person stealing Mr Biscuit's creatures has been selling them for a lot of money. I've been trying to catch the thief by buying them. But I have to take them out of the hollow tree and leave the money, so I don't ever meet him. Now I've come in disguise to see if I can catch the thief when he comes for his money. Do you like my disguise?'

'It's very good,' I said. 'But your moustache is slipping.'

He pushed his moustache back up. 'Ouch!
But what are you doing here, Dougal?'

I told him all about *IhateDougie*. 'And we
know who it is.' Then I told him what we'd put
in the box instead of the Savu python. 'You
see, I got Sybil back, so I don't have to do
what he says any more.'

Mr Wellington looked thoughtful for a
moment.

'I'm sorry about Sybil,' I said, 'but she's
all right now.'

'I know she'll be fine now you have her
back,' said Mr Wellington. 'And I know the
bullfrog, gecko and scorpion are fine too. I
saw your questions on ZooBlog.'

So I told him my cunning plan. And he said it was a good cunning plan. So with his help we carried it out.

We all hid along the bank. Luckily we didn't have to wait too long, because Claude was about to have a sneezing fit.

The person who came to the hollow tree was just the person we expected.

Stan Witzel.

He put his hand in, expecting to find an envelope of money. But what he brought out was a huge and very dead-looking tarantula.

Only it wasn't dead. It was Sybil's skin.

You should have heard Stan yell, it was brilliant. You should have seen his face when we all leaped up over the bank.

'Got you!' said George.

'You creature-stealing fiend!' shouted Burt.

'You'd be in big trouble if you were still in my dad's class,' said Billy.

'Is that Stan's dad rushing over here?' asked Claude.

Lysander Witzel arrived puffing and panting. 'What do you think you boys are doing? Stan, are you all right? Really, you boys should know better than to pick on someone like that. Oh, it's you.' He scowled at me. Then he spotted Mr Wellington. 'Who are you? Can't you control these boys?'

'My name is Wellington,' said Mr Wellington, peeling off his false moustache. 'Ouch! I'm President of the London Zoological Association. I'm the person your son has been selling stolen creatures to.'

'How dare you accuse my son of such things!' said Mr Witzel. 'You can't prove anything.'

'I can,' said Mr Wellington. 'With Dougal's help. And these boys'. But as long as Stan gives me back all the money I gave him for the creatures, I'll say no more about it.'

Mr Witzel handed over a big wodge of money. 'Will this be enough?'

'More than enough,' said Mr Wellington.

Stan walked off with his dad. But as they went, I heard Stan's dad say something to him.

'Good try, son. Better luck next time. Chip off the old block, eh?'

I'M A HERO!

I am once more a local hero. And I'm ungrounded. But I'm still in my room, because I'm spending my last moments with Freda, before she goes off to her new life with Mr Conti. This time I've got Billy, George, Burt and Claude up here as well, so we can all watch her eat a mouse – and have a look at the piece in the bottom corner of page 7 in the *Ocklesford Gazette*.

STOLEN CREATURES FOUND! -----

THANKS TO THE HELP OF A LOCAL BOY AND his FRIENDS, the CREATURES WHO WERE STOLEN FROM OCKLESFORD PET SHOP HAVE BEEN FOUND SAFE AND WELL.

⑦

'Is that all?' asked George. 'I thought you were supposed to be a local hero?'

'It might not sound like much,' I said, 'but Superman never revealed his identity, did he?'

'Neither did Batman,' said Burt.

'I don't think you're Batman,' said Billy. 'Nor Superman.'

'Who are your friends?' asked Claude, who was sitting there with Freda round his neck.

'When are you going to put another recipe on your blog?' asked Burt.

'As soon as I've changed the password again,' I said. 'And you've promised not to tell anyone what it is.'

'Not even Angela?' asked Burt.

'Definitely not Angela,' said Billy. 'She gave the other passwords to Stan. We all know what happened then.'

'What happened then?' asked Claude.

'He stole Sybil!' we all said at once.

'Stan knew where to find our secret key,' I explained. 'From when he lived next door. He stole my trainers. Then he took Sybil. He knew I'd do anything to get her back. But then she moulted and he thought she was dead. So he cut one of the legs off Sybil's old skin to leave in the hollow tree for me. Then Sybil came rushing out of her den and scared him so much he dropped the skin back in. He was so terrified of her that he ended up giving her to Angela and pretended she was her birthday present.'

'So Angela dumped him,' said Billy.

'Can we feed the mouse to Freda now?' said Burt.

I took Freda from around Claude's neck and put her back in her tank. Then I dangled the mouse in front of her with the long tweezers.

First of all she grabbed it and twisted her body round it, all in one super-quick move. Then she held it tight until she was sure it was dead. It was already dead before I gave it to her, but she wasn't to know I'd taken it out of the freezer and defrosted it.

Then she opened her mouth and very slowly let her lips slither over the mouse. Then her whole mouth went over and then only the tail was sticking out. Just like Burt the bullfrog, only much slower.

'Cool,' said George.

'Wow,' said Burt.

'The Savu python has a special hinge on its jaw which means it can open it wide,' said Billy.

'I know,' I said sadly. I'm going to miss Freda when she goes.

MARSHMALLOW AND CHOCOLATE GOO

You Will Need:

- One packet large marshmallows
- One large bar chocolate

MORE ABOUT the AUTHOR

Dougal Trump is once more a local hero!

Method:

Combine all ingredients and put into a warm oven until the smell drives you crazy. It will be all melty and gooey and look similar

241

to Mum's brown goo — but it will taste much, much better.

Inform Mum that you would eat her brown goo if it tasted like this. Dodge out of her way.

Comments:

BigBadBurt said:
Mum won't let me try any more of your recipes as she doesn't want the house to burn down. I would do it while she's not in the kitchen, but I'm not allowed to touch the oven.

BoingBrain said:
I put mine in the oven two hours ago and nothing's happened. I still

can't smell anything. Perhaps
I should leave it in for a bit
longer.

TrussBilly said:
You could try turning the oven on.

Superspeed said:
Delicious.

BoingBrain said:
Mum has just done chicken Kiev and
oven chips. When she brought it out
of the oven, it had chocolate and
marshmallow all over it. It was
delicious and I ate all of it.
I feel a bit sick now.

BigBadBurt said:
Our house filled with gas and Mum
called the fire brigade. Someone
switched the oven on and forgot
to light it. I'm going to have to
evacuate, goodbye.

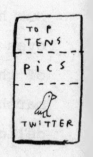

GOODBYE, FREDA, GOODBYE, SYBIL – HELLO, ANGELA!

I felt very sad when Mr Wellington came to collect Freda. He also came to collect Sybil.

'Sybil's going to a good home,' he said. 'To a new zoological collection not far from here. The bullfrog, gecko and scorpion are already there. You can visit them as often as you like. You can get in for free. And Mr Conti says you can come and see Freda any time.'

I tried my best not to look glum. But it was very difficult when I saw Sybil going back into the cardboard box that said *This Way Up*. Mr Wellington let me put her in there myself, by getting her to crawl on to my hand and then off into the plastic container that went inside the cardboard box.

'She'll be fine in there until she arrives at her new home,' said Mr Wellington.

Then it was time for Freda. Mr Wellington let me put her into the box she came in. 'You're very good at handling creatures, you know,' he said. 'Maybe you could work with them one day.'

'Maybe,' I said, still feeling glum.

'Actually, I have something that needs a good home,' he said. 'I've been trying to find someone for a while, because she needs an experienced handler to look after her. But I think you might be just the person. How would you like to have your own horned lizard?'

'I'll think about it,' I said.

After he'd gone, I went on ZooBlog to find out all I could about horned lizards. They like to live somewhere hot, so I'd need a tank with a lamp, just like Sybil's. They live on sand and they eat poisonous ants, which I would have to keep in my room. I like the sound of that. They don't like being handled much, so it's best just to watch them eat their poisonous ants. If they get really upset, they squirt blood out of their eyes. They are supposed to be the ugliest creatures on the planet, but I think they sound really cool.

I told Mr Wellington that I would like a horned lizard.

She's just arrived, together with everything I need to look after her, including a load of big, red, poisonous ants, who live in their nest in a box on my desk with all they need to have a happy life until they are eaten. Mum says that those ants have got to stay in my room or else.

My new horned lizard is grey and bumpy

with warts and lumps all over. She's got a
ring of small horns behind her neck and a
big fat belly. She looks like a mini-dinosaur.
She might be considered one of the ugliest
creatures in the world, but I think she's
beautiful. I fell in love with her as soon as
Mr Wellington told me her name.

   She's called Angela.

CHECK OUT THE DOUGAL TRUMP WEBSITE!

www.DougalTrump.com

You'll find . . . .

FUNNY JOKES

MORE FROM THE DESK OF DOUGAL TRUMP

BRILLIANT COMPETITIONS

FOOTBALL FACTS

AWESOME PRIZES

Don't miss it!